Praise for *Once You Break a Knuckle*

'Combining taut, highly economical observations of men [. . .] with real tenderness and a restrained lyricism about the natural world . . . His characters are tender, confused and painfully vulnerable – romantics, under the calluses, in the Scott Fitzgerald vein, yearning for love and a connection with the world around them, but too raw and frightened to make the attempt . . . Beautiful'
John Burnside, *Guardian*

'D. W. Wilson takes his place with other North American writers such as David Vann and Daniel Woodrell in eking out savage grace and empathy through muscular prose and the desperate circumstances of his characters . . . Throughout this collection, Wilson's prose is whittled down to the bone yet still carries an intense, visceral power . . . An emphatic calling card from a genuine talent. I can't wait to read what he writes next'
Sunday Herald

'*Once You Break a Knuckle*, by D.W. Wilson. Macho Mounties, Boyish Boyz + Beers, Tough Times. + good writing.' @Margaret Atwood

'D. W. Wilson's stories – fuelled by tough, streetwise prose – are alight with tension, wisdom and wit'
Joe Dunthorne

'One of the most gratifying aspects of his debut is the understated way in which he weaves the same characters across his stories, offering, often through the most oblique of glances a glimpse of their fates even decades on. The goes

far beyond mere short-story-telling, creating a vision of entire lives played out against the stifling yet homely backdrop of an isolated community' *Sunday Telegraph*

'D.W. Wilson's "The Dead Roads" was the stand-out winner of the 2011 BBC Short Story Award. My worry was that it might also be the stand-out story in this debut collection, but no – the standard is consistently, astonishingly high throughout' Geoff Dyer

'Canada has a potent new voice in D. W. Wilson. Robust, musical, slyly funny, and shining a fearless light into the yearning male heart, these powerful stories should be required reading for any curious females of the species' Bill Gaston

A NOTE ON THE AUTHOR

D.W. WILSON was born and raised in the small towns of the Kootenay Valley, British Columbia. He is the recipient of the University of East Anglia's inaugural Man Booker Prize Scholarship – the most prestigious award available to students in the MA programme. His stories have appeared in literary magazines across Canada, Ireland and the United Kingdom, and 'The Dead Roads' won the BBC National Short Story Award in 2011. He lives in London.

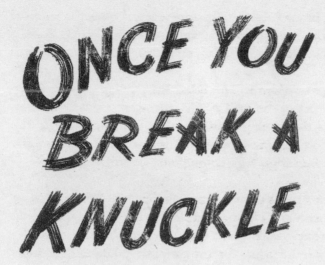

ONCE YOU BREAK A KNUCKLE

D. W. WILSON

B L O O M S B U R Y
LONDON · NEW DELHI · NEW YORK · SYDNEY

First published in Great Britain 2012
This paperback edition published 2013

Copyright © 2012 by D.W. Wilson

The moral right of the author has been asserted

Bloomsbury Publishing, London, New Delhi, New York and Sydney

50 Bedford Square, London WC1B 3DP

A CIP catalogue record for this book is available from the British Library

ISBN 978 1 4088 3131 1
10 9 8 7 6 5 4 3 2 1

Printed and bound in Great Britain by CPI Group (UK) Ltd, Croydon CR0 4YY

www.bloomsbury.com/dwwilson

To Al and Kathy Wilson, and my sister, Amanda,
for their unquestioning, unwavering,
and at times unwise encouragement and support

CONTENTS

THE ELASTICITY OF BONE

On the morning before my old man left for Kosovo, I fumbled along the banister downstairs to the living room, where I found him adjusting his gunbelt so it wouldn't jostle on his hips. He drew the leather through the buckle, notch by notch, and then forced his stomach out; if the belt wobbled, he'd tighten, repeat. He stood a head taller than me and a shoulder wider. His fists were named "Six Months in the Hospital" and "Instant Death," and he referred to himself as the Kid of Granite, though the last was a bit of humour most people don't quite get. He wore jeans and a sweatshirt with a picture of two bears in bandanas gnawing human bones. The caption read: *Don't Write Cheques Your Body Can't Cash.*

When he saw me he cleared his throat, unbuckled the belt, and mumbled about making sure it was working. —You're up early.

I nodded. Beside him, a square foam pad leaned against the couch. He sometimes used it during practice at the judo hall. I gestured at it.

He grinned beneath his moustache. Once, years ago, he had come home from two weeks of training with the moustache shaved, and everyone watched his bare lip with a wary eye. Coworkers hesitated in shaking his hand. Men who were his friends forgot what beer he liked. His sister called him from Winnipeg: *I had another bad dream*.

He hefted the pad and flipped it to me. It was larger than my torso and along the back was a strap for my arm. —Hold it like a shield, he said.

—Why?

—Just hold it like a shield.

I brought the pad up. He squeezed his hand to a fist then let the fingers unroll, muscles tense. Eleven years of kung fu had taught him to strike with the heel of his palm – the second-hardest impact point on the lower arm. He jabbed the bag in quick succession: right, left-right, right, his lips whitened to an *O*, his breath pumping with his arms.

—That all you got, old man? I said.

He flicked his wrists so the joints ground and the fingertips whipped in the air. —Brace yourself, boy.

He coiled his right leg toward his left and held it there, perched on one leg, the arch of his foot nestled around his kneecap. Then he kicked out in a way he had taught me would break someone's knee, because you only need fourteen pounds of pressure to break someone's knee.

I bounced against the closet door behind me and knocked it from its track. My old man doubled over and growled his bear laugh. I pushed the pad toward him. I told him I had to fight in the tournament later. I called him a jackass. He asked me if I had a preference for his right or left fist.

I went into the kitchen and poured myself some coffee. The mug I picked had a picture of one of his friends tending a bonfire with a caption that read, *Burn, Fat Man, Burn*. I put it in the microwave. It was five twenty-seven in the morning and the coffee was already cold.

—Will, he called from the living room, —let's take the trunks to the detachment before the tournament starts.

I told him to wait until I had my goddamn coffee and he told me to get my ass in there or he'd break all the knuckles in my left hand. I told him whenever he's ready he's free to try, so he came into the kitchen and shortly thereafter I was helping him move the trunks. The microwave beeped.

The trunks were police-issue chests fastened with two silver Macedonian locks. The plating peeled around the keyhole and silver flakes speckled the RCMP crests. Letters spelling his name were engraved beneath: JOHN A CREASE. The brass handles left my palms smelling like loose change. We hauled the trunks out, then the boxes from the garage, then the duffle bags from his police room in the basement. He told me to disregard any incriminating evidence I saw about anybody. I asked him what the information was worth to him and he told me pain was a good way to make people agree.

He didn't let me carry the gun. Never has.

We loaded the last of his stuff into the back of the truck – a 1989 Ranger with a rusted door and missing tailpipe. I fiddled with the radio while he fought with the ignition. It was a good truck as soon as you could make everything work. It finally chortled to life and I got some Ozzy playing. The extra weight in the back strained the shocks as we scaled the small lip of our driveway onto the shitty streets of Invermere. The tires dropped into potholes and the trunks rattled in the back.

The detachment was a red brick building that used to be the public library. One of the RCMP cars had a series of stickers on the side that looked like bullet holes; this was fifteen-Charlie-seven, my old man's car. He fingered one of the stickers and peeled it off, stuck it to the trunk, and I threatened to tell the police. He shook his fist at me.

He had joined the RCMP twenty-three years ago and spent all of those posted in small towns on the fringes of B.C. He served seven years in Cranbrook, four in Kingsgate, four in Fort Nelson, and eight in Invermere. This turned him into what he dubbed a *CFL* – a constable for life – since promotion opportunities meant he'd drag his family (me) through shit and broken glass: corporal status, if he'd live in the Yukon; pay increases and living expenses if he'd police a backwater dump he'd have to get to by seaplane, where his son would turn into a user or a gang member and he'd probably end up dead. Promotions, he told me, are a lot like blowjobs: easy to get if you're willing to go somewhere dirty.

Inside the detachment, a stuffed buffalo head hung over the entrance. It was as large as the door of our truck but not quite as ugly. We unloaded his stuff so it could be picked up and flown to the base in Kosovo. The whole peacekeeping thing started when he applied online one night during a Christmas party and proudly proclaimed that he would be going to smite evil. When they called, he couldn't give a definitive answer because he hadn't actually considered it; he was almost fifty, and peacekeeping was a young man's job. But, in short, they'd pay him a lot of money for not a lot of dangerous work: law-drafting and applied police science, no guns.

—You want to get some food before the tournament? he said.

It was by now past seven, which meant the A&W would be open. We ate scrambled eggs and toast and one of their hot apple pie things each, because this was the ultimate breakfast of champions when I was seventeen.

—I've got to be there for opening ceremonies, I said. —I'm coaching the little bastards.

My old man swirled the coffee in his mug, then set it down without drinking. —I'm coaching the not-so-little bastards.

—You calling me a bastard?

—Yeah, he said, and placed his hands on the table, his uneven knuckles enmeshed.

At eight-thirty we went back to the house to get our judo *gis*. He was a black belt, a *shodan*, in judo, kung fu, and kick-boxing, and he had police combat training. I was a brown belt in judo and more sarcastic than him. He wore a Toraki Gold *gi* with a lapel of refolded cotton as stiff as pressure-treated lumber.

5

I wore a Toraki Silver because they were lighter and I relied on speed. He stood six-foot-three and weighed just over two-twenty. I did not.

I slipped into the cotton pants of the *gi* while upstairs my old man got his stuff together. It's important to wear your *gi* before the actual fighting starts, so you're accustomed to its weight and the way the fabric shifts when you move. My old man came down the stairs with his duffle bag in his right hand. He'd changed into a shirt that said, *Pain Is Only Weakness Leaving the Body*, and he'd donned a pair of sunglasses despite the cloud cover, because he liked to pretend to be Agent Smith. I called him that as we entered the truck. He pinned me against the door and used his index finger to roll my upper lip against my nose. For the record, that hurts.

To the untrained eye a judo tournament is distinguishable from a toga party only by the presence of referees. It is a gathering of people screaming at combatants in white pyjamas, a place where redneck wives cough and turn their heads when their husbands grind their hips and paw each other's chests. It is a place of broken arms and vanquished hopes, concussions, overpriced hotdogs, and eastern Europeans.

Our tournament took place in the gymnasium of the local highschool. We'd laid out two fighting areas on the floor, fashioned into twenty-foot squares with red and grey mats linked like Lego blocks. Masking-tape numbers designated them as I and II. Small factions had already formed in the bleachers – groups of eight or ten people rallying under homemade banners that declared *FERNIE ROCKS* or *RAYMOND JUDO*. No fewer than two banners read *CRANBROOK SUCKS*.

Our sensei, Herman, greeted us as we entered. He was an old stonemason from Austria who was once injured by a bomb he'd found in a field outside his home. He'd lain on the ground, his eyes seared blind, a four-inch piece of shrapnel through his chest, for seven hours before help arrived. He was eleven.

When he shook hands he clasped them with both of his. —You made it.

My old man let his duffle bag slide off his shoulder. —I thought about staying home.

Herman pushed him. My old man caught the wrist and tugged. Herman beamed. —You are nervous is all, he said, and nudged me with his elbow. —Your dad is a little scared, just like you were.

—I was never scared, I told him. My old man tapped his fist against his palm.

—When do you leave? Herman said.

My old man eased his sunglasses off his face and held them in front of his chest. I thought about calling him Agent Crease, but Herman wouldn't get it.

—Tomorrow morning. My flight is at ten.

Herman ran his fingers against the grain of his barbed-wire beard. —You will enjoy it.

—I hope so.

—Make sure you check out their judo clubs. It is very popular.

—It won't be the same.

Herman clapped my old man on the shoulder. —It will be better.

He stood there with one hand on my old man's shoulder and peered up at him. The white cotton around his stone-mason's fingers dimpled. He smiled. —But I must go. They are forcing me to ref. We will talk later. Before you go.

Then he wheeled around and moped to the *joseki*, the administrative table, where he was accosted by a pack of men in blazers. They shoved a dress tie at him.

Young *judoka* rampaged around the mats, climbed on the bleachers, shoved each other down and called it practice. Somewhere in this mess of bobbing heads and white belts were the ones I was supposed to coach. A kid I recognized came running off the mat with wet circles around his eyes. He accused another kid of punching him. I told him he could complain when his head hangs off backward.

My old man smiled beneath his moustache. He had put his sunglasses back on.

THE *JOSEKI* SUMMONED me over the loudspeaker. I was screaming like a bookie at a pit-bull fight because the kid I was coaching kept charging his opponent. The other coach – a redneck named Ferman who made his *judoka* call him Sir – was yelling to his kid to use my kid's momentum against him.

I picked my way through the *judoka* rimming each mat and presented myself to the *joseki*. Herman was there with a rolled-up schedule in one hand and someone's misplaced green belt in the other. He told the girl at the table that he had been reffing for the last four hours and wanted a break. She shook her head and shrugged because she really had no say in the matter.

—Sensei, I said. —You called?

He threw the green belt at the girl and tucked the schedule into his blazer. —Will, he said. —Nobody's in your division.

—So split one.

—There's nobody to fight. Under seventy-three is empty. You win gold.

—I want to fight.

—That is too bad.

—It's the last tournament before my old man goes to Kosovo, I said.

Herman tapped his chin with his thumb. —I can put you in the next division. I can put you in under eighty-one. What did you weigh in at?

—Sixty-eight.

He licked his fingers and flipped through registration sheets. —No, eighty-one is also empty. Under ninety. We will put you in under ninety.

—I might as well fight my old man.

Herman fumbled for the schedule in his chest pocket. He held it out in front of him at arm's-length, tilted it sideways. —He is in the senior open division. It is him and one other *shodan*.

—Put me in.

—It is the senior division.

—I know.

Herman crumpled the paper up and shoved it back into his blazer. He was the only person at this entire tournament who would accept this idea. We approached the head table and Herman asked the girl to pencil me in. She told him that she couldn't do that without the consent of the competitors in the category. I told her she could tell the other guy but for God's sake not my old man. She told me it was against policy. Herman told her for God's sake not his old man. He had the green belt in hand again and he brandished it at her. She paged the other guy to the head table.

Judo tournaments grow more intense as they continue. Tottering kids give way to adolescents with a degree of skill, white-belt wrestlers give way to teenagers with the competitive edge. It took hours for the tournament to progress to the masters and the seniors – the old guys who rub A535 onto their biceps and calves after each fight. *Joseki* called my old man's division to standby.

He asked if I'd help him warm up. I told him no problem and he looked at me funny. We started with *uchikomi* and a light *randori* – repetition of technique and a little sparring. He asked how the coaching was and I bitched about it. I bitched about not being able to fight. He told me there were lots of tournaments.

Joseki called, —On deck: Dan Simmons and John Crease.

My old man and I finished warming up. I grabbed him a red sash and told him to put it on. He'd been to dozens of tournaments but never fought in one before, so he was familiar with the details, but things are always different doing than watching. Whoever's name is called second wears the red sash so the referees can identify him.

The Dan Simmons fellow was a black belt in his mid-twenties. Short, clean-shaven, straight hair – he looked like a military cadet who pumped iron to get stronger, not better looking. Probably weighed thirty pounds less than my old man. I watched him do some *uchikomi* against the wall and informed my old man that he would probably try a *seo nage*, a shoulder throw. I told my old man not to be scared. He said if I didn't stop patronizing him he'd make me pay. I warned that idle threats spawn malicious foes. He told me not to quote Shakespeare.

Joseki called my old man and Dan Simmons as "now fighting." I wished him luck.

It was a long, brutal fight. Dan Simmons tried a few tricks by swapping to a left-handed grip midway through. This lost him the match because an opposite grip only works if you are stronger than the other guy, since you're both grappling for the same lapel, and one person is left clutching a paltry piece of fabric on the outside of the shoulder. My old man blocked his *seo nage* with a display of brute force. Dan Simmons was fast – he was young – and he expected to win the fight that way, but my old man is not as slow as he looks. He stepped around Dan Simmons's sweeping legs, his bobbing knees, and though he didn't throw him, my old man, at the end of the match, won by decision.

All in all, a decent first-ever fight.

My old man dabbed his forehead with a yellowed training towel. He squirted water into his mouth from a Judo B.C. water bottle that read: *No Pain, No Gain.* Five straight minutes against a guy half his age was enough to make him see that he was not as young as he remembered. He placed his forearms on his thighs and leaned forward. His back rose and fell with every breath.

Joseki called the two "now fighting" names over the loudspeaker. Then: —On deck, John Crease and Will Crease.

Maybe I'm dramatizing, but the crowd quieted – a third of them, after all, were from our club – and the lights flickered, and my old man lifted his head from his position of crumple and fatigue. He looked at me and I could hear him telling me how I would pay for this when he was a little rested and not as sweaty and after he'd rubbed on the A535. Herman ran toward us to watch the fight. He had that same green belt in his hand.

Then my old man smiled. He dropped his head between his knees and then threw it back and chuckled.

The kids on the mat finished fighting. They bowed off. *Joseki* called: —Now fighting: John Crease and Will Crease.

I stepped up. I donned the red sash. My old man stood and placed his hands on his hips and bent backward. I did my customary hop and slapped the outsides of my thighs. He didn't have a customary opening because this was his first tournament. The ref motioned for us to enter the mat. We bowed and moved to the first line, bowed again and stepped forward. I could see the rise and fall of his chest, the sweat beading on his forehead near the border of his hair. I could almost hear the whistle of his breath through his nostrils. On the sidelines I didn't hear anyone yelling. I didn't look. Never look.

The referee yelled *hajime*.

We are both right-handed. We are both standard grip fighters. I tried to catch his right in my left but he was fast and his massive hand, those massive fingers, curled around my lapel. You only become fully aware of a person's *measure* when you fight him, as though this most base of human activity is the standard by which all people are judged. I clasped his lapel, the sleeve of his *gi*, could sense his patient grip, the complete absence of slack in his arms.

Watching judo is watching two people move in circles until one falls down.

I kicked at his feet a couple times, tried to hook his ankle for a lame win. This pissed him off and he kicked me right back. He was solid and he outweighed me. I tugged, hard, on his lapel and his head bobbed down. I tried to keep him bent over but he didn't like it. He straightened and there wasn't a damn thing I could do to prevent it.

He tugged me and I moved in whichever direction he wanted. He tried to trip me and I stepped over it. Speed and balance. The Gentle Way. I reacted, my feet *fwa-thump*ing on the mat, hooked at his legs, the excess length of our belts whipping around our hips and the red sash some rogue colour among the black and brown. He tugged me again and I moved with it so he put himself off balance backward. This was judo – this was using his momentum and his force against him. Then I was doing my *harai ogoshi*, my Sweeping Hip Throw, and I had all two hundred and twenty pounds of him pinnacled on the fulcrum of my hip.

This was it. He was tired and old and in the air. I was fresh and young and the balls of my feet were balanced on the mat, my knees bent and my calves tensed and quivering. If I threw him hard enough, if I hurt him, just a little – a sprained wrist, bruised rib, minor concussion – he would miss his flight. He would not go to Kosovo. He would stay in Invermere away from the snipers and the land mines, and he would fight me again.

But then I stopped. I was stopped. He brought his policeman's arms down in a bear hug and my balance disappeared. My momentum slouched away. He rag-dolled me into the air and then I was on the ground, pinned beneath his weight, and the referee raised his arm halfway to full, yelled *waza ari*, half-point.

I tried to twist before he could lock it in. His hands found each other and I could hear someone on the sidelines yelling, *SQUEEZE*. He tucked his head down against mine and his sweat streaked against my cheek. Sourness, the split of his lapels. The referee yelled *osaekomi* – hold down started. I couldn't budge him. I hooked his head with my foot and tried to leverage him back, but he just clenched his teeth against the heel in his face. Pain is only weakness leaving the body.

The horn sounded. Twenty seconds done. The referee called *ippon* and my old man's arms slackened. I lay on the ground and stared at the rafters of the gymnasium. A pair of sneakers hung over a metal beam. People on the sidelines laughed and cheered. Herman stroked his Austrian beard, the green belt discarded. Of course it is not fitting that the son should defeat the father.

MY DAD WOULD go to Kosovo. He would be shot by a Serbian man while apprehending him for spousal abuse, something he was doing only because the Kosovo police were short-handed. The bullet would enter his torso just above the second rib on his left side and puncture the lung, and he would feel it compress into a ball the size of a discarded tissue. His fellows would gun the Serbian down, rush my old man to the hospital. They would reinflate his lung and he'd recover.

He would keep the bullet. It is not an easy thing to look at.

Even the referee smiled. I stayed on the ground. My old man laboured to his feet and reached down and I caught his hand. He hoisted me up. He patted my back. The referee awarded him the match and we bowed off the mat.

—Dammit, old man, I said.

—Someday, boy, he said, and grinned, the two of us alone in that roaring gym.

THE PERSISTENCE

The morning he decided to put things back together, Ray walked five kilometres along the highway in the hours when everything was grey except the mountains lightening in the east. It was one of those mean days in November – sub-zero, wet – so he couldn't wear a scarf or a ski mask because his breath would condense on the wool and freeze, and then he might as well have been breathing an arctic wind. It was still dark, five-thirty, but the sky over the Rockies had reddened, which meant today might be one of those days he'd carry with him to the grave – red sky in the morning, sailor's warning.

Ray drew a cigarette from his chest pocket and fumbled it in gloved fingers. He had four, maybe five left, and too little money for another pack. It always bothered him how smoking didn't warm him like he expected it to. He removed one glove to light the thing and burned the ends of his fingers with the match, stupidly, like a fourteen-year-old trying to be cool. Nerves, maybe. This valley, maybe. He'd been absent three years, had spent a little time in Cranbrook, a short stint in Calgary, but the places were deadly similar. Too frequently he bumped into things from the past: a person he recognized, some guy with a sledge seesawing over his shoulder. Relics, anchors. They made him think of *her*.

But all threads lead home, and so does every missing cent and every angry creditor.

The Kootenay Valley stunk of gossip; even the two Calgarians he'd chatted with on the Greyhound were up on local banter, about a cop getting shot in the chest overseas and a tinbasher haunted by the ghost of his dad. He knew people who existed solely for gossip, and given the chance he would bury them all.

He walked under a panelboard sign that read *Welcome to Windermere*. The only way to fix himself, here in this place, was with his old friend Mudflap. Mud had worked with him for five years, started as a dumb apprentice and became the guy who ran Ray's company in his absence. Ray taught him everything he knew, and in return Mud kept him living vicariously. He was the kind of guy who planned his mid-life crisis, whose central philosophy was *persistence beats resistance*. He was also one of the few people Ray had parted with on speaking terms.

Ray found the place after a short walk. Log house, landscaped yard, a couple trucks and a minivan. He was too cold to wait for signs of people awake so he climbed two steps onto the porch and stepped in a pet's dish and something like the haze he'd lived through took hold of him, and he wanted to bootfuck that bowl across the lawn. He'd have to watch himself, avoid people. Mud could help with that.

He knocked on the door and stood straight. People moved about inside. Someone swore and was hushed. A baby cooed.

—I swear to God if it's your dad again I'll kick him in the fucking teeth.

Mud opened the door wearing jeans and a clean T-shirt, a ballcap that said *Olympus Electric*. He had a dad's face now, not age-creased but with skin drawn tight around the bones of his ocular and jaw. His blond wife, Alex, leaned on the wall in a bathrobe, arms crossed and foot tapping. She'd always been a good-looking woman.

It only took Mud a second.

—Ray?

—Hey, Mud.

—Jesus, come on in. You want a coffee?

Ray stomped the snow from his boots. His steeltoes were so damned cold he expected to hear them ring as he set them side by side. Inside Mud's house, he noticed the designer lighting but couldn't say it surprised him – Mud was an electrician, after all. Years ago, Ray worked in a house where the owner, a plumber, had plumbed beer to every sink. Once, he and his crew puzzled over how to wire a swivelling wall in a framer's rec room.

He sat at the table and Alex shuffled to the kitchen to make coffee. Mud intercepted her, caught her forearm, and whispered in her ear. She took the baby and left the room. Mud ground coffee beans and heaped three spoonfuls into the filter and Ray watched his hands. They were the hands of a guy who no longer worked like he used to – not nicked and burred from splinters and construction yards, but still callused. A man never loses his calluses. Well, a working man never loses his calluses. Ray used to tell his guys to find a girl who didn't mind rough hands, and that advice had come to bite him in the ass.

The coffee brewed behind Mud. Ray had taken to drinking espresso because the drip of normal coffee made him lonely.

—This isn't easy for me.

—I know.

—I've got nowhere else to go.

Mud filled two cups.

—Like I told you when you left, Ray. My door is never closed.

Ray wrapped his hands around the mug and felt its warmth. He drank his coffee black, always had. He didn't consume it for fun or flavour, only as a means to keep grinding on.

—I need a job.

—I've got work.

Fucking Mudflap. Fucking reliable Mudflap.

—I need a place.

Mud raised the mug to his lips and held it there. It had a picture of two guys in overalls dancing and a caption that said, *You and Me Soul-Brother*.

—My suite isn't finished.

—You're getting lazy.

—No one to boss me around. Well, someone.

He looked down the hallway toward the door Alex had disappeared through. Christ, she was a good-looking woman.

—A couple days, Mud?

—You got money?

—Do I look like I've got money?

—I see you're bitchy as ever.

—Just old.

Mud pulled his ballcap off and spun it on his finger.

—My suite needs work. You wanna work on it?

—I'd need a place to stay.

—There's light and power and I think I even put up a piece of drywall.

—Are you serious?

—Just lazy.

He'd hoped for a day or two on the couch, enough to get his bearings and find a place with some snowboarder come to work at the ski hill for the winter, a place where he could get jealous of the twenty-something getting laid every night in the next bedroom. A place to make him feel his age.

—When can you start work?

Ray kicked his pack.

—Got my tools with me.

IT TURNED OUT he didn't have all the tools needed, but Mud gave him the things he lacked and a threat that if he lost them, he'd buy new ones. Olympus Electric employed two other journeymen and three apprentices. Mud took one apprentice and gave the rest of the team instructions for the week; they wouldn't be seen except for material runs or if it all went south.

Mud leaned close and spoke in a low voice. —One of them's a woman.

—So?

—I'm just saying.

—Saying what?

—If you want on that crew you just let me know.

Mud winked.

Ray's apprentice, a kid named Paul, sat in his truck in the driveway, asleep against his own chest. He drove a '92 Ranger with green paint peeling to black. There was something sickly frozen in clumps onto the driver's door.

—Is that egg?

—From last Halloween. Fucker's too lazy to clean it.

Mud knocked on the window and Paul jolted awake.

—You didn't load the Bullet?

—I didn't know what we needed.

—Goddamn it.

Paul climbed out of the truck and pulled his tuque over his ears. He was a spindly kid with curly hair and bony cheeks, long arms that could probably haul more weight than a pair twice as thick. He moved with a long, awkward gait; his boots slapped the driveway every time he stepped, as though he hadn't adjusted to the weight of his steeltoes. Mud pointed at the things they'd need for the day and Paul packed them in the work truck, a

'79 Dodge with a metal material box bolted to the frame, aptly named the Silver Bullet. Mud's father-in-law built it for him during his apprenticeship, and as much as Ray made fun of the beast, it held as much gear as a van and burned twice as much gas. It looked like a shed on wheels, and the running gag was to screw crushed beer cans to it, because Mud never removed them.

Ray offered to help load. Mud shook his head.

—It's like obedience training. The kid's got one hell of a lip so I'm trying to breed it out.

—Does he know?

—That, or it's starting to work.

So his days went. In the mornings he'd wake and brew a pot of coffee and make two peanut butter sandwiches, grab his tools, and head out to the Silver Bullet. He'd start the thing so it was warm by the time Paul arrived, always on time. He'd sit in the driver's seat and drink his coffee and smoke while Paul loaded the things they needed for the day.

Mud put him and the kid in charge of wiring a fourplex condo unit. The entire thing was built on two lots, with room on each side; they were tiny, and constructed with each cost cut as low as anyone could get away with. The studs twisted near the tops – culled lumber bought at a fraction of regular price. The place smelled like snow and sawdust and as though someone had pissed in the corner, and someone probably had. He marked the locations for plugs and lights and Paul scurried behind him with one end of a wire spool in his fist.

In the evenings Ray worked on the suite. Mud gave him free rein over the design, access to his supplier for any materials needed, and a budget. Ray added recessed lights over the dining area, a track in what would be a small kitchen after he pulled in the stove. He worked two hours every day. It gave him something to do. He only went out to get groceries, and occasionally with Mud for beers at the City Saloon. He had friends in town, still, and they called him one by one. They wanted to know how he was doing, if he needed anything, if he'd heard any news about Tracey, about her painting company. He'd tell them they'd drink beers and they'd be satisfied, and he'd hang up and press his forehead to the raw drywall and think about how far he'd come, and how far he had yet to go.

HE CAME OUT THE door on a day in mid-December and found most of Olympus Electric's crew gathered outside the shed. They were two journeymen and an apprentice, named Philippe, Clay, and Greg. Philippe was in charge; he was a stubby Frenchman with a white cowboy hat who slurred his *e*'s.

—How's the dumb apprentice?

—He works hard.

Philippe fished into his pocket and snatched a pair of pliers. He started clipping his fingernails.

—You used to be Mudflap's boss?

—Yes.

—And now he is the boss.

He'd been warned about Philippe, the way he'd look down his nose even though the top of his head barely measured to Ray's chin. He had eyes like a pair of gun barrels and he sniffled each time he clipped a piece of fingernail.

Ray lit a cigarette.

—I'm just here to help out.

Philippe stopped with the pliers held level with his chin, his hand half a foot from his face.

—It is good for you then. We are glad to have you.

—Where's Mud?

—In the shed with Kelly. She is angered with me because I try to make her work and she does not. I tell her to bring the things, she does not.

—You make her haul everything?

—She is the greeny. She must do these things.

Mud came out of the shed with Kelly behind him. She had high cheekbones and tight lips bent into a scowl. Her brown hair hung to her shoulders beneath a grey ballcap. She was taller and she wore a denim jacket over a grey vest, and an Usher T-shirt beneath that. She must have been at least Mud's age. Mid-late thirties, maybe.

Mud took his ballcap off and ran a hand through his hair.

—Ray, you have enough work for one more?

—Sure, but no room in the Bullet.

Mud nodded and secured his cap on his head. He strode to Paul's window and Paul started unrolling it, frantically.

—You're driving your own truck today. Bill me for gas.

24

Ray climbed in the Bullet and leaned over to unlock the door for Kelly. She got in and chucked her tools on the seat between them. He snuck glances at her as the Bullet trundled down the highway. She shifted and eyed him, patted the unoccupied middle seat. A curl of dust drifted from the fibres.

—There's room in here for Paul.

—I don't like rubbing up to that kid. He enjoys it too much.

He saw her relax. She put her seatbelt on.

—What do you think of Phil?

Ray wrung his hands on the steering wheel. The windshield started to fog so he cracked his window, thought about lighting a smoke but didn't know if she smoked.

—I think he's a twat.

—He is. Mud's good shit.

—Mud's good shit.

In his twenties he used to cruise around in a shittier truck than the Bullet, Tracey lodged beside him as he tried to shift gears. She'd wear tight jeans, faded on the ass, tomboy. He'd spill his beer and swear and she'd drawl a "whatever" between tokes. She never had trouble fitting in with the guys at work. She was smart, good with her hands, but he couldn't convince her to start pulling wire. She said it'd be too cutesy if they worked together.

—What year you in?

—Just my first. It sucks.

—We were all first-years.

—Not at my age.

—Better than being something lame all your life.

—Like a painter.

Ray startled. He didn't think she meant anything by it, though she probably knew his history. Everybody knew his fucking history. Kelly picked sawdust off her shoulders and arms. She was a good-looking woman, but not in that fire-blooded way Alex was. She didn't make him feel his heart in his chest, didn't make his ears go red. It was different, more subdued.

—Yeah. High from the fumes or the dope in the morning.

It felt good to have a team again. Three guys, a small job. Ray marked instructions on the studs with a fat pen. Paul drilled holes and pulled wire to the breaker panel; he stopped wearing a tool pouch and instead packed his pockets with staples. Ray told him it wasn't a good idea, because those staples would go right into his balls if he fell off the ladder, and Paul started wearing his pouch again. He taught Kelly the basics of circuit wiring and let her finish some that he started. Philippe only had her haul things and dig ditches, the kinds of jobs reserved for highschool kids and idiots who couldn't tell an auger bit from a spade. Paul lingered in the rooms while Ray gave advice, until Ray eventually promised to teach him, too, after they finished the fourplex. Kelly learned fast. She'd be going to school in May, and after she got her ticket, would move to Fort McMurray for a year and work seventy hours a week, leave with a hundred and twenty grand. He'd heard the same thing from hundreds of others, young guys who could afford to work themselves like slaves, old guys who figured they'd last a month, maybe, or land a cushy job as a foreman.

He found himself often in the same room as her. She couldn't keep up to him, but he always managed to find something that had to be finished. A wire too close to the surface needed a nail guard, a light was a couple inches off centre, a few plugs looked too low to the ground so he would have to measure them against his hammer.

At the end of the day she asked if he wanted to come for beers. Ray slung his belt into the Bullet. The first condo had already been drywalled.

—I gotta work on the suite. I took the day off yesterday.

—It's only a couple beers.

—Next time.

Paul looked up and for the first time actually held Ray's gaze.

—You sure you don't want to come?

—I said next time.

The kid knocked on the window of his own truck and Kelly opened it from inside. Dumb bastard only locked the driver's door. Ray got into the Bullet and lowered the window so he could smoke. The Bullet couldn't play music. Mud used to haul ass from site to site with a portable stereo plugged into the lighter and bang his head to tinny rock and roll.

THE NEXT DAY, as he pulled up to the fourplex, there was a brown van parked in one of the driveways. The side of it read *Excentuate Painting*.

Three years ago he'd found that same van, or at least one like it, at the mountain resort he'd been contracted to renovate. His company, Straightline Electric, had to refurbish the condos; the job was to swap minor things like yellowed faceplates and broken light fixtures, work nobody wants to do even though it pays well. He'd been on his way home when he saw an Excentuate van parked at one of the places he'd renovated. Excentuate Painting had been, and still was, owned by a guy named Caine – not the smartest or the nicest, but the kind of guy who knew when and where to buy the beers. Tracey had worked for him but quit when he hired a team of highschool kids to blast through the houses as fast as they could – a kind of fuck-it-we'll-fix-it-later type approach.

Then, at that resort three years ago, Tracey had come out of one of the condos. She saw him in his truck as he rolled by. She waved. He'd pulled over. Caine came out the same condo a second later.

—Afternoon, Ray. How are things?

Tracey sidled up to the truck and opened the door. She hopped in as though he'd come to give her a lift, as though everything were hunky-dory.

—I might go work for him again. He fired the highschoolers.

After that Ray started asking around. It turned out Tracey spent a lot of time with Caine, and everybody knew it, so one day Ray pretended to go to work and instead sat outside his house in Mud's Dodge. Caine picked her up in that same van and Tracey welcomed him inside. Ray timed it and could conclude nothing. They came out with coffee mugs. Tracey insisted they were making coffee. Business, she said, always business. Then, on a Friday evening, while Ray drank beers on his porch and watched his dog play, Mud came tear-assing down the driveway, chewing gravel in that Dodge. He stepped down, decked out in his Carhartts and steeltoes, all tans and browns, looking like a man with a secret to tell.

And now, that memory still fresh, Ray couldn't go inside the fourplex. He pinched the bridge of his nose and tightened his grip on the steering wheel. There had to be a way for him to escape without freaking the hell out of Kelly and Paul. But he couldn't leave them alone, either, or that'd be Mud's ass.

—You alright, Ray?

—Need a second. Twenty-six-ounce flu, you know.

He didn't think she bought it, but she gave a nod and stepped out of the truck and started unloading. Paul asked what was going on and Kelly shrugged. The kid lingered for a second; Ray could see him in the rearview. He wanted to bark at him to get to work but he didn't need to. They unloaded everything and began without instructions. The painters were in the first condo. They'd be warm and doped out of their heads and wouldn't wander out to the cold or into the unfinished basements. If he stuck to the ground and to the open air he'd avoid them. He couldn't see Tracey today. He wasn't ready for that.

Kelly appeared at the window, but before she said anything, Ray opened the door. He grabbed a spool of wire and his tool belt and trudged into the basement of the last condo, as far away as he could get. Kelly carried two electric drills and a fifty-foot extension cord.

—We starting on this one?

—I am. Finish up over there.

—It's not pulled yet.

—Pull it. If you get in trouble ask me. If Paul finishes the feeds, show him how to tie in.

He set up his wire spool and plugged in a drill and bored holes through studs and the floor joists overhead. The way the bit curled into wood satisfied him, always had – that hint of heated spruce in the sawdust and at the tip of the metal. He never minded wood chips in his hair and never wore a ballcap to keep them out. Ray'd use sawdust-scented shampoo if such a thing existed. At lunch, Kelly brought him coffee from her thermos while Paul waited in the Bullet. She wore pink mittens over her work gloves that she kept hidden in her lunch kit next to her thermos. Half a sandwich dangled in her hand. She turned the wire spool on its side and sat down. Ray sipped the coffee. It was nearly white from all the milk and way too sugary.

—You need any help over here?

—I'm doing okay.

She bit her sandwich and shoved the food to one cheek as she spoke. —You wanna come for beers tonight?

—Floyd Flannerly's Christmas party is next weekend. We can have beers then. And they'll be free.

—I can never take that guy serious.

—Because he's a plumber?

He offered her the coffee and she washed her food down.

—No. Because he actually wears flannel shirts, she said. She stood, brushed herself off, and saluted. —Too cold. Going back to the Bullet.

He watched her pick her way across the cluttered floor. Her boot caught his extension cord and she had to kick it free. She saw him looking and stopped, her foot three inches above the plywood ground, one hand wrapped around a stud for balance. She looked like the girls on the front of tool magazines, brand-name drills held upright at their shoulders like guns. Except Kelly had a sandwich and not a drill, and heavy grey overalls instead of skimpy shorts.

Tracey used to wear a massive winter coat, open so she could reach the tools in her chest pockets. She preferred wool gloves that left her fingertips exposed, with flaps in case it got too cold to bear. Her hair was blond and ear-length; she had pucker marks from years of smoking, a few wrinkles around her eyes – nothing unattractive. She had been raucous on-site. In the winter she packed a halogen work lamp wherever she went, for warmth rather than light. She was known for being terrible in finished houses, would carry things twice her size and mar the walls, damage the ceilings. It was the way she thundered around the job site that drew him, the way she moved antithesis to everyone else. She would stomp over a pile of debris rather than skirt it.

Kelly shook herself free. She flashed a grin, bit into her sandwich. He dipped his head in a nod and she turned and disappeared.

LATER THAT DAY HE damn near drilled a hole in his leg. Paul gave him a lift home because Kelly didn't have a licence, and Ray couldn't operate the clutch. The kid drove with the speedometer not wavering from one hundred, as though Ray would give him shit for going too fast. When they got to his place, Paul stood awkwardly at the passenger door, his arms half-extended.

Ray limped out of the vehicle, turned and faced him.

—You want a hug or something?

—Was thinking a kiss, actually.

Ray grinned. The kid knew how to throw shit after all.

Inside, he opened a Kokanee and sat on the couch. It was times like this when he wished he had money for cable, but he barely had enough for shitty beer. He raised the can and drank half. It tasted like the stuff he used to drink in the States – *real* manly, *real* light – and it reminded him of raised trucks and shotguns, a twenty-year-old drywaller named Burt with a backward hat and a stomach that drooped over the edge of his tool belt. They hunted coyotes along gravel roads, so drunk they could barely see. Then Burt shot one and it didn't die. Ray wanted to finish it but they left it with its final howls rattling in its throat.

He pulled his pant leg over his calf. The drill had only glanced along the meat without boring into him, but it had winched the fabric so tight the muscle was bruised and bloodshot. He flexed it and it ached. Not the worst injury he'd ever taken; in fact he'd be able to work tomorrow, dammit. It was only eleven. So much for the four-day weekend.

Someone knocked on the door. He yelled that he'd be a second, and started to work himself to a stance, but his calf seized and he fell onto the couch.

—Fuck it. The door's unlocked.

Alex opened the door and peeked through. Her hair was up, but a few strands hung down the side of her head. She had a bag of ice tucked under her shoulder and a small black film canister in her hand.

—I got a call from Mud. How bad are you?

—Not bad enough.

—I've got ice and our secret stash of T-3s.

—I'll take the ice.

Her hands lingered on the edge of the door before she closed it. She wore track pants and a windbreaker, had probably been out running – one of those fitness women with legs like nautical rope. A film of sweat shone on her forehead and she placed the back of her wrist to it, let her eyelids drop. Her shoulders rose, fell. Then she stalked across the room and extended the ice.

Ray took it, careful not to let their fingers brush, and wedged it under his calf. Alex hesitated near the coffee table, arm's-length from the couch. Ray set his beer down.

—Where's Madison?

—With my folks.

She toyed with the zipper on her jacket and didn't look at him. He'd known her longer than he'd known Mud – she waitressed at a restaurant he frequented during his apprenticeship, too young to be taken seriously, labelled an up-and-comer by the sleazebags he worked alongside.

Then, when he took Mud under his wing, she always came with him to the parties and gatherings, this crazy, mysterious blonde you could tease but never touch.

—You want a beer?

She shook her head. He scratched his stubble. Fifteen years, maybe more.

—Well. You alright, Alex?

—Can I sit?

He shifted his leg off the edge of the couch, moved over, and shoved the ice up along his calf. It stung his damaged skin. She sat on the lip, far opposite him, and stared forward. He reached for his beer but it was too far away, so she grabbed it by the rim and slid it to his palm. He felt like an idiot and drank the rest and Alex looked at her watch and then set her hands on the flat of her thighs.

—You've known Mud as long as I have.

He could sleep with her, right now, if he wanted to. That's what she was going to tell him – that it'd been a long time since Mud touched her. He'd seen it before, hundreds of times; guys get so infatuated with the new business that they neglect their wives and then their wives go and sleep with fucking painters who get doped each day before work.

—Mud's good shit.

She drummed her fingers on her knee.

—You ever get tired, Ray?

—All the time.

She turned her palms upward and stared at them, one then the other. They were small and soft, hands that could

34

easily button up a shirt, hands that didn't grapple power tools. When he did the same, Ray saw only twenty years of scrapes and cuts and decades gone to waste. But Alex read something in her own, or read something in his. Or, more likely, she simply saw right through him. He had no idea what she wanted.

Her eyes fixed on him, those raven lashes, those irises as bright as sparks.

—Sure you don't want the T-3s?

—Save them for when I drill *through* my leg.

—The suite looks good.

—Bedroom's the nicest so far.

She scrunched her nose as though recoiling from a bad smell.

—Do you ever get tired of, you know, this?

—All this?

—I don't know.

She crossed one leg over her knee and leaned her chin on her wrist. She was such a good-looking woman.

—It's hard not to. It always seems like everything's the same until the moment when you *need* everything to be the same. Then you find out it's been different the whole time.

Alex bobbed her head. She drew a strand of hair from her face with her pinky. The nail was groomed, curved perfectly around the fingertip. Ray smelled cinnamon, assumed it came from her; the scent of a clean body. She rolled one eye toward him, her face turned only a degree in his direction.

—I knew about Tracey and Caine, before you found out.

—Everybody did.

—I'm sorry I didn't tell you.

Ray shrugged. —Nobody did.

Alex went to the door.

—Are you going to Flannerly's party this weekend?

—I promised Kelly and Paul that I would.

—Paul looks up to you.

—Only because I don't rail on him like everyone else.

—It's more than that.

Ray shrugged again. Alex cocked her head and the tie on her hair loosed, dropped that mane all the way to her biceps.

—You regret coming back?

—Not one bit. Other things, yeah. Part of being human.

—Man from beast.

—You regret me coming back?

That got her out the door. Before she closed it, she peeked her head in.

—What if Tracey's there?

He'd been mulling that over since he'd agreed to go. Worse than Tracey, he feared she'd be there with Caine and that he'd say something dumb and get in a fight. Caine was ten years younger and he went to the gym every second day. Ray couldn't afford to get the shit kicked out of him. He'd lose everything, again. And he couldn't blame *everything* on the two of them.

—Hopefully I'll be too drunk to realize it.

—Have a gooder, Ray.

She shut the door. He struggled to his feet and fished another beer from the fridge and nursed it on the couch, counted the hours. Ray'd mulled over other stuff, too: where to go when Mud eventually gave him the boot, how long he had until his body at last failed him, whether Kelly was *actually* giving him the eye. It wouldn't be a stretch to say a certain kind of woman caught his attention, but it wouldn't be a stretch to say that scared him cold. Kelly did things the way Tracey used to, a no-bullshit approach that he admired and made a show of admiring. But she had rough edges, too – he'd seen the way she scowled at Philippe – and a past Ray would one day have to ask after. He didn't know her story but he bet he understood how she felt: everyone who falls off a roof usually lands the same way. And if she *was* attracted to him – if he didn't, for instance, need someone to pull his head from the clouds – then Ray knew why: broken people are drawn to broken people. That's the love life he had to look forward to with Kelly: a three-legged race.

Not that it'd slow him, not that it'd sway him. Ray would persist. It's just what he did.

EVERY VEHICLE IN THE driveway of Flannerly's shop was a truck. He spotted Paul's Ranger and pulled the Silver Bullet – the only vehicle he had access to – in beside it. A group of guys smoked outside the shop. Ray recognized one as a lippy plumber named Ben, but the others he didn't know. He stepped out and nodded. A black Lab bounded from among the trucks and put its nose in his hand.

The plumber, Ben, waved his cigarette at him.

—Hey, Sparky.

Ray gave a deep nod. —You talking to me or the dog?

—The dog's not a goddamn electrician, is he?

—He'd make a hell of a plumber, though.

Ray winked and went inside. Flannerly's shop was a giant shed, wired with heating and a television upstairs, unfinished walls, material piled in the corners. The walls were dressed with *Playboy* tear-outs and posters of girls in swimsuits. It felt like any other shop Ray had ever been in, except six times as big.

Some thirty guys and a handful of women sat in a giant circle. They had two barrels of iced beer and a table with whiskey. Ray set his bottle of rye on the table and poured himself the first glass. Rye and Coke, cut one-to-one. He found Mud and Paul and joined them. Paul nodded and Ray clapped him on the back. The kid wasn't so bad.

Mud passed him a beer.

—Guess I'm double fisting.

—Ray, Kelly started eyeing you the second you walked in.

—I like Kelly.

—You should. She's a coug. I'd hit that if I wasn't married.

Ray winked.

—How much you had, Mud?

—They call me Doctor Love.

Ray shot the last of his rye and took a beer from the stash Mud had beside his chair. Paul sat smiling and mute; his stack of empties was only half as big as Mud's, but he was doing his best. Bunch of drunken idiots, the lot of them.

Ray spent most of the evening trying to work up the courage to go talk to Kelly. The night wore on. Mud entertained the group with a story about bull riding in Kelowna under the name Texas Dunlop. Some cabinet guy tried to breakdance but slipped on a crushed beer can and twisted his wrist. At one point Mud leaned toward him, elbow in his ribs, and nodded at Kelly. She had gone to the liquor table and stood apart from everyone else.

—Persistence beats resistance.

—I'm not sure that applies.

Mud nodded, sage-like. —Ray, it always applies.

He joined Kelly at the liquor table. His rye was the least touched of all the booze there, still half-full. He lifted it and filled a plastic cup halfway and offered it to her. She took it. He filled his own and they stood, side by side, but not looking at nor talking to each other.

—How'd it go after I drilled myself?

—We're not going to talk shop, are we?

Ray shrugged, beaten. —Couldn't think of a way to get started.

She tapped the table with one finger and left it resting there. —Can you drive?

He shook his head. —Not legally.

—How'd you get here?

—Illegally.

She left her drink on the table and slunk to the exit. She stopped in the doorway, pressed to the frame, her Usher shirt visible through the cleft in her vest, and winked. Mud saw the wink – had to see the wink – and put on a *go for it* grin. When Ray looked back she had disappeared except for the tip of her hand. Her fingers waggled on the wood; the nails were chewed down. His ears went red, and not from the booze. He went out the door. Behind him, the guys gave a cheer.

They walked to the beach because Ray couldn't drive, and it was about as romantic as things would get, boozed as they were. It was darkening; the sky over the Purcells had turned a milky red. Red sky at night, sailor's delight. The frozen lake creaked, giant ice plates ground like earthquakes, once so loudly she jumped. They leaned against each other. He felt like a sixteen-year-old anxious to get laid. He stopped noticing things, tripped on tiny rocks and almost ate a mouthful of sand. A tree branch, bent and loose like a drunk's weighty arm, took him straight in the chin. She laughed; he cursed and swatted.

Their meandering took them to the far end of the beach where the sand terminated against a concrete wall. Above them loomed what remained of a wooden fort, weathered to a mottled rib cage lined with insulator's plastic. A long time ago it was a ferry port, when people traded up and down the Sevenhead River. Ray used to party in it as a kid, had his first blowjob there, pressed into the corner with a bottle of rye in one hand and a fistful of denim jacket in the other, jeans drawn down past his ass.

Kelly gestured at the fort.

—I slept with a twenty-two-year-old there, last year.

—Wish I could say the same.

From her vest she produced a silver flask, held it flat in her palm with one thumb curled over the spout. She flicked her hair around to the other side of her head, showed off the curve of her neck, a mole perched on the cusp of the jugular.

—It's chocolate vodka.

Ray let her churn the flask in the air beneath his nose, leaned forward as if to follow when at last she retracted it. It smelled like a coffee house, like dark beans or maybe the liqueur they squeeze into brandy chocolates. When she tipped it to her lips he watched her swallow, her neck again.

He wanted to reach for her hand and lead her away.

Her house was a few blocks away – the basement suite of a thirty-five-hundred-square-foot house. Two other girls, half her age, lived there too, but they'd gone home for Christmas. It was almost, she said, like having a place of her own.

The chocolate vodka didn't last long. It was the first step in losing their clothes, there in her well-lit bedroom. Kelly slid her hands around his grey-haired chest, over his gone-soft biceps, and Ray stared at nothing but that bedroom light – how could he turn it off without being obvious? But, perhaps sensing the unease in his stiff, trembling shoulders, she flicked the light so he didn't have to. Then, for the first time in three years, he kissed a woman.

Soon after, naked under the covers, he plucked a bolt of lint from her belly button and she giggled. Kelly's body disappeared beneath the blankets, her muscled legs only shadows against the curl of his palm. Ray caught a glimpse of himself, his pasty gut, his mangled hands on her stomach – how could she be genuinely interested in him? With this awareness went his boozy haze, and, with that, everything that mattered at a time like this. He focused on Kelly, the sound and sight of her, the way she shifted with his hand and tongue.

He thought of Tracey, followed the memory of curves and moans and the way she would sink her teeth in the soft of his ear. But Tracey was not the woman laid out beneath him; his memories did not match the curves, the sway of breasts. He imagined how Alex would've acted at a time like this, or how he would've acted with her thighs sticky against his jaw, those muscles that must reach like taut ropes toward her knees. Christ, she was a good-looking woman. His old body hovered above Kelly, spread along the length of her, limp. His lips grazed the coarse hairs between her legs but it didn't matter, nothing was going to matter.

Ray rolled off her and sat on the edge of her bed. One of her legs touched his lumbar beneath the sheets. Amber light from a street lamp leaked through the tiny window; it blanketed his feet and lit his discarded pants. She shifted. The blankets rustled. He wouldn't do this well with a woman ever again. His cock dangled against the bed. The sight of it made his cheeks hot, made his fists ball. Kelly fidgeted behind him. If only she would say something.

Then: a hand on his back, between the shoulder blades, warm in the winter cold. He imagined the contours on

42

those fingers, the nicks and scars and the chewed nails and he felt a tingle, down there, but it lapsed as he noticed. He shivered and leaned away; her fingertips lingered on his spine.

A real man would save face, blame the booze, answer with bravado and nonchalance – but Ray had long moved beyond that. You get less and less invincible, he figured. Or you give up trying. Years ago he would have demanded a blowjob and passed out halfway through. Instead, he hooked his jeans with his big toe, slid them toward him, and tugged them on. Her hand disappeared. The denim balled at his kneecap.

—You can stay, if you want.

He did want. He wanted so bad to stay there in that bed, sexless and warm, snug against the tight muscles in her lumbar. He wanted to wake late with his face buried in her hair and watch her dress in the blaze of daylight, naked and his, even for just this once.

—I'm sorry. About this. It has nothing to do with you. So much depends on this night and I don't know. I don't know why.

He felt her shrug.

—So go to work on Monday and tell them everything they need to hear.

Something like relief passed through him, a great exhalation. Ray lay down with his arms at his sides and clutched the blankets. What was there for him to say? It felt like highschool, the first time he ever had sex, the winces and squinting eyes, cold sweat on the bedsheets. Kelly coiled around him. Her warmth spilled into his backside; the human body produces as much heat as a one-hundred-watt bulb. Ray let the night happen. She prodded his feet with her toenails and, later, laced her fingers through his. He didn't flinch. He didn't even shiver. All the problems could wait.

SEDIMENT

In the last weeks of the school year the hallways empty out and summer gets so close you can taste it like iron in your throat. Invermere, the whole town – maybe all of B.C. – is suddenly the eye of a desert storm. The wind kicks dust down the main haul but there's not a soul, not a tumbleweed, only this feeling in your gut that you're shooting on through. My days blur into report cards and administration and the occasional phone call to a student's mom. Ceremonies, grad pranks, a party in some teacher's backyard with a bonfire as big as a motorhome. It's euphoria, it's like a thing earned, and the hours swelter by without worry over recompense.

But you never quite move on from what you've left behind. At night, on my porch, I eat grapefruit wedges and think about who got me here. The air smells like the mountain wind and the citrus juice pooling on my plate. Life is a series of events between shitstorms, or so my dad used to say. On the porch, I'll imagine Bellows, the only guy who ever bared his teeth for me, his bob-and-weave walk, his messy hair and that grin more bucktooth than lip. Then I'll remember the hick, Ham, huffing on the asphalt, his breath sticky with hops and his mouth full of blood and sand, how bad he looked after Bellows beat him pulpy. And for a moment I lose track of myself: there's only the grapefruit and the valley wind and the questions that will trouble me to the end of days.

WE MET AT THE end of our grade eleven year when Ham, this highschool dropout with a pigskin face, caught me late for class. He pinned me to the school's stuccoed wall and waved a bony fist under my nose. —This is what you get, he said, and pushed the knuckles against my nostrils. I was a hundred and five pounds and Ham had one fat arm across my chest. He stunk of chewing tobacco, wore an nWo ballcap turned one-eighty, a button-up denim coat. I was a teacher's boy, the kind of kid rednecks take a fancy to, and I generally spent my free time hiding behind the tungsten-coloured portables, in a cubby someone had hollowed in the earth.

I smelled that jagged fist and imagined how bad Ham would smash my face with it, but then Bellows, a Jehovah's Witness with biceps bigger than my neck, came out of nowhere. He threw himself at Ham, this tornado of arms and grunts and spit. Afterward, he brushed dirt off my shoulder and asked if I was alright. —Yeah, I told him. —And thanks.

Bellows was new to town, said being a JW often caused him trouble in Christian settlements like the Kootenay

Valley. *Settlements* – he used that word, I remember. He had dog-brown hair and freckles and a mole beside his nose. Having him around felt like having a police escort. His family had moved to the valley from Manitoba, where his dad worked as a mechanic for a JW community outside Winnipeg. Bellows claimed to not touch alcohol and he was forbidden from eating ketchup or having sex out of wedlock, but rumours said he and a girl named Charlie tried it in the backdoor. He had one green eye but the other was colourless grey. His dad could refute the theory of evolution. I once saw him curl a one-hundred-pound dumbbell in each arm, and that made him the stuff of legend, like a figure out of the WWF.

We killed time together at lunch hour in a walled-off courtyard accessible by a door marked *Staff Only*. The stucco was algae-green with a shin-level strip of sandstone brickwork. Bellows only ate peanut butter sandwiches and a grapefruit, quartered, and he always offered me one of those wedges and I always accepted. For the first time in four highschool years the hicks hesitated to pick on me and for the first time since he could remember Bellows had a friend who didn't care that he was a JW. I showed him the dirty hollow I used to hide in and he collapsed it with two great guillotine-stomps. He read me a couple verses from his Bible. We hiked Invermere's main haul and he bristled whenever we passed anyone who might cause trouble. A couple times he thought somebody was making a move and he went stiff, pupils dilating and his heart a-thump like a kid in love.

At the end of May, Bellows found an ad in the newspaper selling a '67 Camaro, so we drove to a town called Edgewater to have a look. When we got there, the car was on cinderblocks outside a mobile home – cobalt blue, darker than the desert sky, rust-peppered tinwork. Bellows lowered a palm to the frame like worship. He lifted the hood to stare at the V-8. When he blew across the engine, dust coiled into the air, thick with the smell of carbide. We tried the doorbell but all we got was a Rottweiler's blood-howl, so deep and throaty it left you scratching your chest for an itch, and we hightailed it out of there. A few days later Bellows took me to his garage, and perched amid the clutter and the freezers full of elk meat was that beautiful Camaro. —My project, he told me.

Summer got into swing. Beach parties, valediction, a gathering at the gravel pits where guys shotgunned cans of Hurricane like it was coming into style. Me and Bellows spent so much time in his garage that we missed the big happenings around the valley. Some kid wandered out of the gully at the edge of town. A retired highschool teacher signed up for the MMA Tough Guy tournament and shattered a student's nose. Us: we tinkered with the Camaro. Bellows flung me tools and crooned instruc-tions, and for the first time in a really long time I thought life was going alright. At home, my old man asked me what the hell I'd been getting up to, and I just told him, —Tweaking that car, Dad, and he gave me the eye, as if to say, *Is that all?* The whole time, Ham drove loser laps along Invermere's main haul and we saw him with a puck slut riding shotgun, a giant decal on the tailgate that said: *UR2SLO*.

In July Bellows fired up the Camaro for its virgin run. His dad helped us with the guts but when we repainted the body Bellows made a point of it only being me and him. Afterward, the cobalt drew the eye like an athlete. We cruised around in that beater-on-the-rise. Bellows pushed a Queen album in the tape deck and we blared "Fat Bottomed Girls." People gave us looks. At the only red light in town we sidled up beside some hicks in a raised pickup. Their bass drowned ours, but Bellows gave them the eye. They called us fags, and he revved the engine. Then the light greened and Bellows dropped the clutch straight to second and I made a paddling motion out the passenger window as we shot on by.

Near the end of summer me and Bellows swung by the lake, just bombing around, desperate to scrub up excitement. On the way, we bumped into his friend Charlie, wandering home with a bottle of Crown Royal. She crammed between us – athletic, brown haired, with nice teeth and a smile that showed her molars. At the lake, Bellows parked the Camaro under a street lamp and we hiked with Charlie to the water to circulate the booze. We sat on the sand with our shoes off, dipped our feet in the lake.

—How much that car cost you? Charlie said. She gave Bellows a look, a once-over. I'd have traded anything to be in his shoes.

—About two grand so far.

—You ever wonder, she said, but didn't elaborate. She tapped her feet against Bellows'. Their knees brushed. The water swam with sediment. I had Bellows' shoulder wedged against mine but I thought I could smell Charlie – the scent of citrus fruit. I'd have given anything to switch places with Bellows.

Charlie dangled the Crown Royal between her thighs.
—I can't drive stick, she said.
—It's just timing, Bellows said.
—You could show me.
—Yeah, if the time's right.

He never closed the deal. Charlie offered him more whiskey but he had to drive. Out of courtesy she offered me some and I tried to taste her lips on the bottle. Then we heard boys yell and tires screech, and when we looked at the Camaro there was Ham's truck and a bunch of guys scrambling out of it. Bellows straightened. I caught Charlie's eye and I could see that she wished I were not there. Bellows took off in a sprint. By the time he reached the parking lot the hicks had scratched *Fucking Fag* across the Camaro's hood with a key.

Ham was halfway inside his truck when Bellows heaved him to the asphalt and kicked him in the ribs, hard. He grabbed Ham's hair in one fist and cracked him in the nose, and cracked him again, and again. Other hicks climbed from their truck but one glare from Bellows made them wait it out. The whole time Ham blubbered like a kid being beaten. He was saying sorry. He was saying he was so sorry.

When Bellows finished, Ham's face was puffy, as if by bee stings. He went fetal. Bellows had blood and snot on his knuckles and teeth marks in the bone and one hand had swelled to the size of a ten-ounce boxing glove.

—Call someone, he told me.

—Bellows? I said.

—*Call someone*, he said again, this look in his eyes as if he meant *help me*.

Bellows' parents didn't take well to the news. In a few days his dad made plans for him to hash out his last school year in Manitoba, at that community for JWs. It was August. Town slowed to a drift. Summer jobs ended and kids hit the streets to meander their dwindling freedom. Me and Bellows did what small-town boys do. We got shitfaced on cheap vodka and pinged rocks off coal trains. We made half-hearted attempts to score girls. In the dirty hours of the morning, with the sun cresting the Rocky Mountains, we traipsed down the street and discussed anything except the fact of our parting.

In four months I'd be in the thick of my grad year and Bellows would join the Canadian Forces, take his knuckles overseas to the sandblasted Afghanistan dunes. There, some iron shrapnel would open his throat like a quartered grapefruit and he'd see God as things go blue. I'd graduate at the top of my class, and on the evening of convocation Bellows' old man would show up and pat us all on the shoulders. I'm still not sure why he came – to look for ghosts, maybe, or to hang on to something. At the end of the night he caught my arm and hissed, —You were everything to him. A decade later I'd need a new electrical panel and the electrician turned out to be Ham, clean shaven and ready to make a name for himself. —Whoever woulda thought? he'd say to me.

But that's summer for you. Or, that's summer for me. These nights are short, and some evenings I sleep and wake and dream, here on this porch, until the sun lifts over the mountains. Bellows was the only guy who ever bared his teeth for me. Even my dad, rest him, never had the stones. When night recedes and the dawn turns cobalt, I shuffle inside and put music on to make it sound like there's somebody home. I pour myself a drink. There are probably a few things left unsaid between me and Bellows, but that ship, as my dad used to say, has run aground.

This is how me and him say goodbye: on the eve of his departure we climb into the Camaro and blaze around the gravel pits with the headlamps dark, and we bawl and laugh and hug and skid donuts until we've kicked up so much gravel it's like a sandstorm passing in our wake.

THE MATHEMATICS OF FRIEDRICH GAUSS

I've never been very good with my hands. Sure, I can swing a wood axe or heave on a pry bar, but ask me to pluck a suture or shuck an oyster and I start trembling like a man afraid. My doctor told me it could be nerve damage to the wrists – I got jackknifed in the birth canal – but I'm more inclined to believe I just never learned dexterity as a kid. My dad could've spun a few stories about how dangerous I am with a chop saw, or a hockey stick, or his prize fillet knife that once tasted the grit of human bone. It's why I became a math teacher. Clumsier than a stiff clutch, my dad used to say.

My wife knows the truth of it. She's the only reason I can walk into the bar here in Invermere and not get snickered at, the reason I can smoke salmon and pull-start a chainsaw, the reason I can, but rarely do, heft a firearm. She has red hair, darker than mine, but she knows how to wear it. In summer her skin turns statue-bronze and her veins push to the surface like a boy's. At rest, her curls tease the divot on her chin where, as a child, she barrelled into a brass doorknob. She's got excess bone on her hip. One earlobe hangs a quarter-inch shorter than the other, and in the evenings when she thinks I'm dozing she'll stand naked before our bedroom mirror and examine her body's faults. It's as if she worries that somebody expects something more. But I've always loved her nicks and notches. I am a fan of her inadequacies. Like Carl Friedrich Gauss, the Prince of Mathematics, I am in love with a woman who outclasses me by spades. Behind every great mathematician, and all that jazz.

It's 1994, the International Year of the Family, but my wife has left town to hike the Rocky Mountains. She's gone to muck her way to an unnamed peak southwest of the valley, where she'll pitch camp and listen to elk bugle below her and where she'll sip the homegrown chamomile tea she's packed among her clothes. It's a chance for her to get some distance from Invermere, B.C., from the people who mutter for hours about our scabby streets and all the driveways kibbled by snowplows. It's a chance for her to remember that the world exists somewhere else.

Me, I'm building a heliotrope. My son's idea. He drew a list of supplies and found a diagram in his science textbook, and now I'm expected to piece the thing together for him. There're two reasons he chose this device. First, because it's April, the end of term, and his grade four teacher, Barry Rogers – who everyone calls Wingnut on account of his ears – decided to go small-town-America and host a science fair. Second, because a heliotrope looks not unlike a laser rifle, my son wanted it mounted in his tree fort. It's a survey device, actually, used to reflect light great distances. Gauss, my hero, invented the heliotrope and used it to triangulate the border of northern Germany. Nineteenth-century surveying involved men of uncertain sobriety waving paper lanterns in the night, and Gauss loathed to see things set aflame. The heliotrope's a simple design: tripod base with a mirror and two monocle lenses that you beam sunlight through, to make a signal that is visible for miles. The whole contraption affixes to what could pass for a telescope – the old, bronzy type that colonels sidearmed during the American Civil War.

My son and I are not alike, at least not physically. Colleagues crack jokes about mailmen and the uncertainty of my loins and I do my best to not let suspicion eat me. I've got fibrous red hair and a jaw tapered like a rugby ball. In my prime, I once benched a hundred and forty-four pounds, which, within acceptable variation, I've weighed since grade twelve. My son, though, he's got a working man's brown hair and this scar from earlobe to eyebrow where, as a toddler, he sliced himself on a nailhead. Takes after his mother, and that's alright, except for his disposition toward fighting shows, which he comes by quite honestly from me. Each day he and the neighbour's boys blitz home to watch the Power Rangers on my forty-two-inch rear-projection TV. This happens at three-thirty, Monday through Friday. I bring them some Coke they split amongst themselves and a bowl of dill pickle chips. On commercial breaks they gossip as though running out of time: there's a new kid in town whose dad's a cop;

the Cooper children wear patched-up jeans because their parents can't even afford heat; some teenager got arrested on the playground for selling parsley to the elementary schoolers as dope. And I sit in the kitchen and eavesdrop. I do it because sometimes it's hard for a dad to understand his boy, but also out of loneliness and a sense that nobody has friends like those we cause mischief with as kids. It's a chance to feel my own childhood, a chance to think about just how unhappier I could be.

I've heard misery skips a generation. My dad was a heavy-duty mechanic who got his thumb jammed in the door of a Peterbilt Class 8. It took two miles for the driver to notice him running alongside, if you're to believe what my dad had to say. He called that kinked thumb *the rachet* because it tended to buckle out of joint in fifteen-degree stutters. Gimped or not, he was one hell of a mechanic. Once, he used crochet thread and two bulldog clips to jury-rig a Volkswagen Beetle that'd snapped its accelerator hitch. Another time, on the highway to the Prairies, I watched him repair our Ranger's exhaust pipe with leftover ringwire and a good helping of machismo. I'm pretty sure he wished I'd wear a boilersuit alongside him, but handiness with machinery is one marble I did not shoot. Dad used to say I'm a few knockouts short of a punch, whatever that means.

I'm writing a biography on Gauss, because I like to think our lives are similar. Gauss's father was a stone-mason named Gerhard who planned for his son to wield a beechwood mallet and slop his hands with mortar. Gerhard dreamed of founding a man-and-boy masonry called Steinbrecher und Sohn. In the evenings, he imagined, he'd drink *Roggenkorn* and bicker with Gauss over *geschäft*. That's all the German I speak. No pictures remain of old Gerhard, but with a name like that you can bet safely on a square jaw, handlebar cheekbones, and an ocular ridge with more angles than the Grand Canyon. Gauss stood five-foot-two and stocky like someone accustomed to hauling brick. A workman's build. His father's son. In letters, his colleagues always mention Gauss's blue eyes. Portraits of him show an unremarkable, squat man with chops a frontiersman could abide. His nose is stout and curved at the end like a knuckle. One thick eyebrow arches, tantalizingly, and he smiles like a man who has discovered a secret we're all dying to know but don't quite have the nerve to ask after.

Anyway, it's the end of April here in Invermere, which means, among other things, that the frost has turned to dew and the lake has thawed and somebody has won a couple hundred bucks guessing the day the ice went out. It means evening light shallowing toward the horizon, the mountains casting long shadows across the valley. Kids, like my son, sense the approach of summer and get antsy from a winter spent too long indoors. Teenagers discard their shirts too early. Firepits are re-dug and lawn chairs trawled from toolsheds and for the first time in months the neighbourhood smells like woodsmoke and hotdogs roasted over open flame. Wives complain about too many coat hangers unbent to sausage spits, but not much can be done about that.

I'm in my backyard with a couple empties and the salvaged scraps of a weathervane. I've got a grade four science textbook spreadeagle on a cinderblock. My wife's toolbox yawns atop our picnic table, red and blastworn like a fire hydrant. This year, as I said, is the International Year of the Family, but my son is out of town on a class field trip to Banff. I'm building him a heliotrope anyway, because I'm bored and because I'm a good father. The sun has slunk toward the Purcell Mountains and its light scatters through the planks of my lumber fence. My wife built the fence – it took her a whole evening just to trowel holes for the posts. I offered to help, but she said I was a schoolteacher, not a fence builder, so I stayed indoors and drafted lesson plans and watched her through the slatted bedroom blinds. She wore a muscle shirt with sweat-stained ribs and jeans faded in great smiles at the thighs. Each time she shovelled, her lips peeled over her gums and I imagined the breath that trilled between her teeth. Back then, I knew the sounds she could make. Periodically, I mixed rye and Coke and gave it to my son to ferry out to her. She told him: —You could show your dad a thing or two about how to treat a lady. He repeated that line around the house for days. He was four years old then, and wouldn't have known what she meant. Nor would he have noticed the tension each time he said it, or the way my wife cringed like a woman who had come just shy of having the life she dreamed of as a girl.

IN 1805 GAUSS MARRIED his first wife, Johanna Osthoff, a tanner's daughter he'd known since childhood. As kids, the two of them built hideouts among the sweetgums and peat bogs feeding into and out of the river Elbe. Some nights they snuck from their homes. Johanna helped Gauss climb trees – he was a short boy, but he had strong arms – and Gauss guided her gaze around the night sky. As an adult, Johanna liked to read and she liked her own fierce individuality. Her favourite novel was *Ardinghell and the Blessed Isles*. If she were living right now, she'd open a used bookstore across the street from Chapters, she'd sip chamomile tea with friends named Chakra and Peaceflower, and while her husband crunched numbers and found the dimensionality of fractals, she'd lead protests and rear a family whose politics would shape our future. She had the hands of a woman who would know how to operate a belt sander. When clean, she gamed with the scent of wild animals. Her fingernails were chewed to beneath the quick, and Gauss, to a friend, would one day confess that he looked upon those gnarled nails with a sense things had come and gone. When he knew her as a child – even, perhaps, when they first became romantic – he remembered her hands as lithe and delicate as a babe's. But Johanna's hands were never soft; for years she'd helped her old man at the tannery, bucking leather and scraping rawhide with a scud. You see, what Gauss remembered was how he'd *imagined* her hands to be. When we're young, we overlook our lovers' inadequacies, and the true test of companionship comes when we must weather those inadequacies through eyes grown wise by age and disappointment.

I met my wife at a lake near Saskatoon when she was nineteen and fleeing. I'd just dropped out of university because of a girl named Austin who had tar-coloured hair and a droopy eyelid that always made her look tired. My wife was cross-legged on the beach with a bottle of rye speared in the sand, a box of matches on her knee. She'd sparked a fledgling campfire. I had a messed-up head and a 1969 GTO that reeked of early-twenties angst. I asked my future wife if I could help her set up camp. At first she said nothing, just tied her hair in a crimson ponytail that caught the sun's light like a bottle. Then she sent me for kindling, and I chopped wood until my shoulders pearled with sweat, until the sun hung like a dollop on the horizon and the tarry Saskatchewan dirt was gummed beneath my nails. We built the fire and hit the rye and didn't say a whole lot.

That was sixteen years ago. Things worked out. I spent a year pouring forms and wrestling concrete and after doing that in the howling Regina winter I'd had my fill of the workforce. I graduated with honours in mathematics, returned for a teaching certificate, and eventually landed a job here, in Invermere, heart of the Kootenay Valley, far from the maddening prairie flats. But it's been a learning curve – I was a city boy, unversed in the nuances of rural life, the divide between rednecks and bluecollars, the gestures and conventions everybody takes so seriously but won't spend a minute to explain. Kids use words like "ratbag" and "minkstuffing." Men shrug, unworried, when their sons learn to drift at the gravel pits. Fights break out in the school parking lot, and the more robust among us wade into the throngs to haul the combatants apart. My wife, bless her, has dragged me through it. Sixteen years now I've sped along in her wake. She's managed to start her own renovation gig, and together we've raised our son to be someone into whose care you could entrust a belonging.

I am thirty-eight years old. My wife is thirty-three. It's 1994, the International Year of the Family, but, while I rig this heliotrope in the backyard, my wife has left town to see a trade show in Calgary. She's gone to admire Hilti watersaws and the latest in laser levels, to visit a couple cowboy bars and grind across those skid-marked floors in snakeskin boots. She'll be wearing her red hair so it dangles to her shoulders, and she has this way of pulling it behind her ears to expose a mole on her collarbone. It's all a means for her to let off steam – I'm not exactly the portrait of an Adonis. Every now and then I put her on edge: she'll groan at the way I drink my coffee; she'll lock the bathroom door when she showers; she'll come home from work smelling of sawdust and exertion, but no coaxing can lure her to bed. Lately, I haven't seen her naked much, and she's always exasperated when I do, as if I shouldn't be so excited, as if we were a goddamned teenage couple without all the benefits of being teenagers.

But the heliotrope. The science fair. Like I said, it was my son's idea. Most of his classmates have opted for traditional science fair gigs: his friend Duncan has concocted a baking soda volcano; another boy, Richard – who has a glass eye – is doing a spinning Cartesian diver; one kid, apparently, plans to build a replica particle accelerator that smashes marbles together like atoms. If my son were here he might have a shot at convincing me to do something more grand, something to be proud of, like a small-scale homopolar railgun. I'm not too upset that he's away. I don't like him to see me drink, and I've had one or two tonight, I've had one or two one or two times. He's out of town, with his mom or with his soccer team, it doesn't really matter.

Gauss would have known where his children were, every hour of the day. He had six in total, two-thirds of whom survived to adulthood. For a man of his accomplishment, he sought modest futures for his offspring: marry a good woman, have good children, be a good dad. He abhorred the thought that they follow him into mathematics, but not for selfishness or even underestimation of their intellect; rather, Gauss foresaw the rise of the working class, of people like my neighbours who respect jobs that build things, jobs with a weight you can test against the strength of your arm. Only his eldest, Joseph, took this advice. The others fled to the new world, the frontier, to carve their way among the prodigal sons and daughters who waged war on the Confederacy.

A week ago my son had his first real run-in with the locals. I mean the hicks – the right-wing gun toters who exploit our unemployment system, who pop welfare cheques on dope from the Native reserve, who think beef jerky and Coke constitutes a decent lunch to pack their kids. Their children are the type who shatter Kokanee bottles on semi-trailers, who pelt windshields with clumps of clay big as potatoes, who find genuine humour in the suffering of others.

It was recess, and a group of these cockroaches had trapped a grain-thin boy in the school's red spiral slide, and they were taking turns battering into him boots-first. Well, my son walked by and my son stepped in. The hicks administered him a lesson in numbers. It marked the first time he reamed a blow off his forehead, the first time a nurse at the brick hospital had to sew him up. My wife removed the sutures three days later – I'm a tad clumsy – with a delicacy I didn't know her tradeswoman fingers could muster. She braced her hand on his forehead, wrist across his cheek, and I knelt nearby for encouragement. She smelled like drywall and the hemp-oil salve that labourers knead into their palms. After she plucked the last stitch from his eyebrow, she swabbed iodine on her thumb and massaged it over the gash like mothers do in movies from the fifties. —There, she said, grasping him at both shoulders. —You're fixed up.

We stayed up late that night, my wife and I. I had marking to do, and a new assignment to concoct, and together we soaked our worries. It felt as though we'd come out of a bath. You might call it a dark hour. Invermere, despite the blaring inadequacies, for a long time had been our haven, and I don't think either of us felt ready for the approaching weight of our son's adolescence. My dad used to say they toss the manual out with the placenta, but I sense even that joke is a relic of time slipped by. Nowadays, you'd get a manual drawn in the multilingual cartoon way you see in aircraft safety leaflets. I'm only half kidding: what good will the values my dad beat into me do against a generation unfazed when one of their own ODs on PCP, against kids who pawn their parents' electronics for coke money, against the advent of meth labs and pushers who market it as a good way to stay thin? These are the things that loiter on the horizon. You don't have to be a mathematician to put two and two together.

My wife sat beneath a hotel blanket. She had a rye and Coke on the bedside and she clutched at our ancient tortoiseshell tabby. I had a few Kokanees – comfort beer. My wife looked old. In the incandescent light her red hair was yellowed as though by cigarette smoke, and the creases at the corner of her eyes were deep and rigid. All the wrinkles around her mouth curl downward. She has, through no fault of my own, spent much of her life frowning. Like all of us, she has a past: when her dad died, she thumbed it, penniless, to the Prairies, and you can guess how she paid her way; her brother took the family car on a joyride to a logging camp in northern Manitoba and hasn't been heard from since; she has an ex-husband – a marriage that lasted sixteen days, one for each of her years. She only tells me these details when she drinks whiskey, and she only drinks whiskey on occasions like Christmas or a long weekend or the day that could have been her anniversary.

So that night, a week ago, I slurped beer suds and racked my brain for questions a grade ten kid could puzzle through. My wife sipped from a ceramic mug that had a picture of the two of us hoisting a trout. When she finished her drink, she rattled the meltwater ice cubes, and I shuffled to the kitchen to fix another. A good husband must do something kind and unique for his wife every day. Nothing else makes sense.

—Ever wonder if we could've done better? she said when I came back.

—We've done okay, I said, and passed her the drink, which she took in both hands like an offering.

—I want him to stay like he is. A boy. I don't want him to be like us.

—Like me?

—That's not what I said.

The day after we met, on that beach near Saskatoon, my wife showed me how to gather barnacles for protein. She shanked a pocket knife between the rock and the shell and popped the creature off like a coat snap, this grin on her face like nothing in the world could be more fun. I never got the hang of it. She has stopped showing me how.

—We're not unhappy, I tell my wife.

—Don't you ever wonder if you could have done better? she says, and she looks at me with eyes grown wise and disappointed.

Gauss's first wife died in 1809, complications from childbirth. A number of people have recounted the scene at her deathbed – how he squandered her final moments, how he spent precious hours preoccupied with a new puzzle in number theory. These tales are all apocryphal. These are the tales of a lonely man. Picture them, Gauss with his labourer's shoulders juddering, Johanna in bed with her angel's hair around her like a skimmer dress, his cheek on the bedside, snub nose grazing her ribs. He'll remarry, yes, and love his new spouse. He'll father three devout middle-class sons unafraid to scull for their lot. He'll become a mathematician scholars name when they talk about the Big Five.

But picture him, the Prince of Mathematics, as he closes Johanna's eyes with his stumpy, working-class hands. Things he notices: her immaculate, cream-coloured fingers; the dint on her eyebrow from banging it on a grandfather clock; the wallpaper they installed themselves, herringboned and crooked near the ceiling where he had to balance on his drafter's bench. And Gauss suddenly realizes the whole place smells like chamomile tea. Maybe it's too much for him. He needs a drink, which will become a pattern – one or two gentleman's glasses while he idles, sometimes more when the missus takes the boys out of town. His face puckers at the edges, not tears, but fear. He can't know what will happen next: and what is more terrifying to a mathematician than the unknowable?

It's 1994, the International Year of the Family, but my wife is crossing the Rockies, or browsing a trade show in Calgary, or driving a 1969 forest-green GTO south to the American border. If she's in the Rockies, she's got her sister with her; she's fucking a twenty-four-year-old cowboy, Gus, if she's in Calgary; and if she's on the way to the border then she's tucked my son beneath a yellow hotel blanket, because she's taking him away from here, away from the drudgery he'll suffer as a boy in a small town, from the hockey louts he'll fall in with and the mill job he'll get locked into and the girl he'll drug with Rohypnol in 2003. And I'm in my backyard. I'm building a heliotrope. And it's well past dark and I've been drinking, I won't lie. I've been drinking. See, I don't know where my wife is. I don't know where she's taken my son. But I do know I caused it, I've done something wrong – because I'm a man, a mere math teacher, and I have certain specific inadequacies, none of which are the fault of mathematics.

RECEPTION

I spent the winter break of my graduating year alone with an aging tom. It was a year when Invermere suffered heavy snowfall in time for Christmas, and the city plows combed the streets in a way that left great palisades across the driveway. Each morning I chipped at this barricade with an aluminum shovel until I'd carved a gap my truck could squeeze through.

Weeks ago everything had gone to shit. Lightning split a tree in the front yard and magnetized all the electronics in the house, including the clocks, so it was always one thirty-nine that December. Mitch Cooper, a long-time buddy, cracked his house's foundation when the clutch of his family's Jeep caught in first gear, and it'd be years before his folks let him live that one down. Then my old man took a bullet to the chest in Kosovo. Twenty-three years in the Force and he'd only twice gone without his Kevlar. His lung collapsed. The doctors at the base reinflated it, pried the bullet out, and sent him home. He was on a plane back, or on a train to get on a plane back, or in a car, on the road, in a country, driving fast, to get on a train, to get on a plane back. The RCMP wasn't one-hundred percent. But they'd let me know.

It was three weeks between when my old man got shot and when he returned. In that short time, relics of him appeared around the house: I found an instrument for testing grip strength wedged under a couch cushion; the cat knocked a silver RCMP tie pin off the fridge; downstairs, a canvas punching bag, worn and sweat-stained at the midsection, ripped from its ceiling hook. I fired up the uninsured Bonneville in the garage to see if the damned thing still worked, and the inside smelled of shaving cream and Old Spice deodorant and a trace of spilled beer – it smelled like my old man.

Months earlier, I'd driven him and that Bonneville to the airport in Cranbrook, a shithole city best described as a place even the hicks think a bit too small-town. My old man squashed into passenger with only a duffle bag for luggage. It held three items: his electric razor, his judo *gi*, and a balled-up gold chain the Force wouldn't let him hang around his neck. He wore his dark glasses and a black T-shirt that read: *You Can Run, but You Can Also Scream*.

The Bonneville's dashboard looked like the heads-up display from a space fighter, complete with a wire-frame model of the car that changed from green to yellow to red as parts broke down or took damage. My old man watched the speedometer the whole way and if I notched it above one hundred he'd threaten to commandeer the vehicle. I warned that if he didn't stop heckling me I'd drive over a cliff. He said all it would take is one good punch to the neck and I'd be out cold. I asked if he meant the head and he just slapped his fist against his palm. Then he made a call on his cellphone, to his friend Darren Berninger, and told Berninger to be without mercy in busting me for speeding. In fact, my old man said, one eye levelled at me through dark glass, be a little unfair.

We talked about upcoming movies and he asked me to send him a DVD of *The Bourne Supremacy*. I offered to mail him the cat. He respectfully declined. At the airport, a young security guard with nervous hands detained my old man for a key chain fashioned like little handcuffs. They could be used as thumb traps, the guard said. To cut off a person's thumbs. My old man deadpanned the poor bastard and said if anyone actually got caught like that, they didn't deserve thumbs.

On the night he finally returned, my buddy Mitch came over.

It was late by then, dusk. From the couch I could see the yard and the road through the front window, and Mitch pulled up in his oxblood Rocket 88. He didn't drive that car in the winter if he had a choice since the street salt could threaten the undercarriage. It was a 1953 vintage beast, a car more attitude than metal. Mitch's old man, Larry, purchased it from some hick twenty years earlier. Larry was a birdwatcher by trade, the kind of guy who could wear a coonskin hat and not as a joke. With fifteen thousand dollars and the patience of a birdwatcher, he teased that car from ratbag to beauty.

I met Mitch at the door. He wore a leather jacket and some leather gloves and a grey scarf. I'd known Mitch since I was eight years old. He was all long arms and bony knees, had a terrier's bouncy eyes. A scar dented his cheek where a pebble got embedded when, at the age of ten, he crashed his bike into a yard umbrella. He stood six-five, shorter than he'd end up, but I barely topped his collar. When we were kids I made him look spindly, but he'd filled out, lifted weights, ate enough for his parents to joke about making him pitch in on the food budget.

—How's it going, Will? he said. He didn't take off his coat or his shoes and he didn't step out of the entryway.

—You okay? I said.

He shoved his hands in his pockets, rolled his neck and let his shoulders lower. When he stood like that he looked like the right kid to pick on. But I had seen those shoulders pulled back. I had seen him bare his gums. —Just tired, he said, and moved his arms in a way to flex his chest, his biceps. —Been helping my dad clean the windows. Fucking hicks egged them again.

We went to the kitchen. I offered to make him coffee and he accepted, even though it was well past dinner. Once, in tenth grade, Mitch bought an espresso machine for his room and shotgunned three solid cups, and I guess the caffeine mainlined to his brain because he charged out the front door. Hours later he returned with a limp and a sprained ankle and mud stamped across his chest like paw prints.

—It'll be good to see your dad again, Mitch said.

—He left a message a few days ago. He's in transit.

—How is he?

—Mostly angry, I said, and Mitch grinned like a boy.

I put only enough water in the pot for two cups. Mitch toyed with the salt shaker – a canister painted to look like a cop's pepper spray.

—My dad wants to have you guys over, Mitch said.

Steam lisped out the coffee maker and I waited for the drip. Mitch set the shaker down. Larry wanted my old man over for dinner to talk about the hicks, and my old man would oblige him, because we'd all been friends so long.

Mitch exhaled and his breath hung dewy in the air.
—It's really cold in here, he said.

—I don't have the heat on too high.

The placemat in front of him was crooked so he straightened it. —You'll freeze the pipes.

—I won't freeze the pipes, I said and waved a hand at him.

He went to the thermostat and cranked it. As the baseboards heated they filled the kitchen with the scent of old metal. —Your dad will sleeper-choke you if those pipes damage.

—He could *try*.

—And then he'd sleeper-choke *me*.

I gave Mitch his coffee in a mug that showed a picture of Darren Berninger poking at a fire with the busted end of a Calgary Flames hockey stick. The caption read: *Burn, Fat Man, Burn.*

Then headlights flashed through the living room drapes and Mitch and I went to the window. A patrol car pulled into the driveway. The RCMP drove white Impalas with push-bars on the fronts to buffet deer and motorists who'd decided to run the gauntlet. Fake bullet holes stickered the hood and the driver's door – it was my old man's car, fifteen-Charlie-seven, the same one he'd driven for eleven years.

Mitch's Rocket plugged the only shovelled entrance to the driveway, so my old man had to plow through the snowbank. The car shuddered quiet and my old man climbed out, all two hundred and twenty pounds of him assembling beside the car. He slung a duffle bag over his shoulder. He shut the car door with his boot. Dark glasses covered his eyes and he wore a blue winter coat, open, and he hadn't shaved his moustache as a matter of family luck. The RCMP crest was emblazoned on his breast.

My old man doesn't walk. My old man doesn't saunter. He picks a destination and he *wills* himself to that destination. But, in winter, the front yard had a defence: a lone rosebush with its limbs laden and limp over the icy walkway. My old man was fixed on the front door and I guess he didn't see the rose stalk that swayed at eye level because he collided with it at a pretty good tilt. His head snapped back and his hand went to his face and the duffle bag hit the ground. Years later, he'd blame the glasses but I'd point out that it was his fault for wearing sunglasses at night. He'd tell me that if I broke into song he'd punch me in the ribs. I'd break into song. He'd punch me in the ribs.

Mitch and I looked at each other. My old man's cheek went bright red and his nostrils flared like a stallion's.

There was a maroon welt in the fleshy cove beneath his eye. He dabbed blood with his thumb.

The bastard cat sagged off the couch and stood beside us. I grabbed a tissue from a box on the gimped coffee table my old man and I had accidentally split in two down the middle. The door opened and he stepped through and I offered him the tissue. He pressed it to the wound. The cat mewled. I've heard it said that cats talk to humans more than they talk to other cats, even in the wild, as an attempt to domesticate us. My old man blinked at the cat and growled; he would not be domesticated by the likes of that tom.

Then: —Son.

We hugged like men. He was leaner than I remembered and he didn't squeeze very hard. Later I would realize the significance of that, of the open coat which, closed, would snug too tightly over his bruised chest. The duffle bag slid off his shoulder and he eased it down without bending his torso. When he removed his coat I saw his Kosovo Force T-shirt; it showed a bandana-wearing bulldog chained to a wrecked wall:

KFOR

If you can't run with the big dogs,
go sit in the food bowl.

—How's it going Mr. Crease, Mitch said. He extended a hand.

My old man clasped it and he and Mitch stared at one another, eye to eye. To this day, Mitch is the only friend I have who will hold that gaze. —It's still going, Mitch, my old man said. —How's your dad?

—He's my dad.

—Amen to that.

—He wants to have you guys over, Mitch said.

My old man held on. He and Larry got along well enough but they came from different worlds. —Well, you guys just let me know when.

—Tomorrow night.

—Alright.

My old man tossed his coat onto his shoes and inspected the house. He remarked at the poor state of each room. In the den, fingerprints gummed the computer screen and the wood stove was grainy with charcoal. Did I even bother to vacuum? Is the cat still shitting behind the goddamned toilet? I told him I'd followed his instructions and not wrecked the house and what did he expect, leaving an eighteen-year-old in charge for six months?

After the inspection he dug into his duffle bag and revealed two liquor bottles the size of champagne flasks. The corks were secured by duct tape and the bottle swam with the colour of morning sky. Inside each was a wooden cross, swollen so its ends brushed the glass and *tink*ed when my old man handled them. He hefted one in each fist.

—Rakia, he said, pronouncing it *rock-ya*. He set one of the bottles above the fridge in the liquor cupboard. —You didn't drink all my booze?

—You told me not to.

He unwrapped the duct tape from the second bottle and uncorked it. Then he fished three short glasses from the cupboard and lined them up.

—Sorry, Mr. Crease, I don't think my –

—Have a drink with us Mitch, my old man said.

The liquid he filled each glass with was the colour of watery eyes. It smelled vaguely like pears and churned with wood pulp. He handed one glass to me and one to Mitch and then he raised his own.

—To coming home, he said.

The rakia tasted like a pinecone dipped in rubbing alcohol. Mitch, poor Mitch, was red faced and coughing after just a sample. Mitch drank coolers if at all. I could feel the liquor all the way down and my old man told us the trick was to hold your breath and swallow at the last possible instant.

—It's bottled by nuns, he said as he downed what remained in his glass. He held up his index and thumb barely apart, as though pinching a nickel between them. —They put this little cross in each bottle and it swells. You're both sissies.

Later, after Mitch left, my old man and I sat on opposite couches watching the dark television. He was half-covered by a blanket and lying where the cat would normally curl up. The bastard creature perched on the back of the couch, waiting for its chance to move in. A glass of rakia nestled on my old man's chest. The cat wouldn't look at him but he made faces at it.

He tipped the glass up and let a mouthful of rakia slide

down his throat. I watched him swallow and exhale a long, slow breath. —This is watered down. Me and Lou couldn't even handle one shot of the stuff before they bottle it.

—What about the nuns?

My old man winced and I don't know if it was the rakia or not. —The way I see it, son, never get involved with a woman who can drink you to the floor.

—They're nuns.

—That's not the point, he said.

—A nun drank you to the floor.

—That's not what I said.

I threatened to tell the other cops that he had been out-drunk by a nun and he threatened to acquaint my skull with his fist. I said I had nothing to fear from a man who was floored by a nun and he said if it wasn't for the goddamned cat, who would take his spot as soon as he stood up, he'd show me why they called him the Kid of Granite.

—You didn't think to get the TV fixed? my old man said, after a time.

—Insurance is supposed to come look at it.

—You have to pester them.

—I've been a little preoccupied, you know, you getting shot and all, I said.

—*You've* been a little preoccupied?

I dropped silent at that. We didn't talk for minutes. My old man was not supposed to be the type I could scathe. I picked at my fingernails and he sipped at his rakia and then the cat padded down to his torso and my old man yelled out – a deep, throaty sound like a winded man huffing his breath on the dirt. The cat leaped two feet into the air and yowled. My old man sat up, bent in two, the last swallows of his rakia spilled on his shirt in a dark *V*. His hand clenched his chest, under the left breast. The fabric dimpled around his fingers.

—Dad? I said.

He rocked back and forth. I can't remember a single event in all my life as awkward as those moments when I stood helpless in front of him, hands tensed at my sides, his eyes squinched shut and his jaw clamped and Jesus, what had this done to him?

THE NEXT MORNING I woke to my old man cursing, followed by a crash and what sounded like a body crumpling to the floor. I had the only basement bedroom, half-tucked beneath the stairs. A tiny ground-level window overlooked the backyard and, if not for the snow, the tips of the Rocky Mountains.

I sat on the corner of the bed and worked myself to consciousness. My old man swore after a second heavy *thump*. Then he was pounding on my door and telling me to wake up and I was telling him to stop pounding, for the love of God. I opened the door. He wore a pair of black shorts and an old pink workout T-shirt with red lettering that said: *I Sleep With a Pillow Under My Gun*. There was a bulge under the fabric at his left breast.

—You need to help me hang the punching bag.

—What time is it?

—If you go back to bed I'll wake you with ice water.

I said I locked my door. He crossed his arms and shrugged in a *you think that'll stop me?* way.

In the rec room downstairs, my old man kept a set of free weights and a treadmill and a Total Gym exercise machine. I preferred the free weights but he refused to let me use them without a spotter, threatened to bust out his taser if he ever caught me doing so. The punching bag leaned on the wall and the workout bench was cocked at an angle toward one side of the room. He'd tried to balance the bag on the bench while securing it to the hook, and though it was an admirable strategy in theory, there was no way for him to lift the bag, balance it, and climb up alongside.

I told him I wished I'd seen him try that.

The two of us squatted to heft the bag, arms low and knuckles against the floor like apes. Our fingers dug into the underside of the canvas. He counted to three and we heaved and he yelled for me to use my legs and I yelled for him to lift straight and after the bag fell sideways a second time my old man pushed me away and told me to just wait on the bench.

Once he stopped heckling me and held the bag still, it didn't take long to mount. The damned thing was older than me and yellower than sweat and I have no idea what it'd been filled with. My old man practised a few jabs, a quick succession of right, left-right, right. He wore leather workout gloves that made your hands smell like old dollar bills. The bag shuddered with each impact. He fell into a rhythm and struck it only on its downswing, hard enough to jerk it backward with unsettling human-like recoil.

—You want in on this? he said.

We used to train together, one of us on each side of the bag, alternate our punches, like tetherball. His hits always landed an elbow's height above mine so the bag hourglassed between us. It was a game: try and back the other guy up, force him to circle. I often had to circle.

—You sure you're good to be doing this?

He was already a little red cheeked. With every hit he loosed a sharp breath.

—Scared? he said.

I strapped on the extra pair of gloves. Nylon, shitty.

He'd taught me to throw my punches on that bag, in third grade when it became clear I'd need to know how to defend myself. —Some people don't like police, he'd told me as I mimicked the placement of his fist, the flex of his biceps, the precise curl of his knuckles. —They'll tell their kids to pick on you. Only fight if you have to. You'll probably have to.

Before he threw a punch he'd draw his elbow to his hip, hold it tensed, and then he'd lash out and his body would half twist and his wrist would turn one-eighty in the air. With each strike his neck muscles corded and I saw his jaw clench, his teeth grind. His fists *whump*ed the canvas. The bag juddered, buckled on its chain, and I met it with all the momentum I could muster, over and over, until sweat shone on our arms and faces and my knuckles ached and my old man's breath wheezed in short gulps like a man sucking air through a straw.

THE PHONE RANG FOR most of the day but he only answered twice: his sister in Winnipeg who wanted a day-by-day account, and who refused to hang up until my old man promised to make a photograph slideshow, and Darren Berninger, who was throwing a party as a way to welcome my old man home and as a way to get smashing drunk. Every off-duty RCMP member would be there.

Shortly before dinner I drove my old man downtown so he could reinsure the Bonneville and procure a flat of Kokanee from the liquor store. Our truck was an '89 Ranger with a bench seat so filthy he nearly refused to sit on it, because he had standards and because he was no savage. But he could still fight like a savage, he warned, so don't try anything. I told him real men sleep on beds of earth and only shower when it rains. He said if I wanted to lay my face in the dirt he could help speed the process, and then he tapped his fists together, twice. Outside, the sky had already darkened with December twilight – gone sheetmetal grey – and he asked if I'd seen any decent movies lately. His T-shirt read: *Cops Only Have One Hand – the Upper Hand*.

In the evening we hiked it to the Coopers' house rather than drive, even though the journey would take a good twenty minutes, because my old man didn't want to risk having his car ratbagged by the hicks. He'd decided to advise the boys at the office about Larry's vandalism problem, and I asked if that would help, and he told me they'd get what they deserved.

—Maybe Mitch and I should just hunt them down.

—I'm thinking this prey isn't worth the bullets.

—It only takes one, I said.

In the distance, the top of the Coopers' house appeared over my old man's shoulder. He planted himself and turned toward me and his lips bowed at the corners – a slow grimace – and I wondered if his chest ached, if he could feel the hole where the lead pierced in. And then I regretted saying anything at all.

—Seriously, Will, he said, and seemed to look past me. He favoured his left side, even just standing. Dark lines circled his eyes and bled to wrinkles. The welt on his cheek widened like a grin. He could've been anyone's dad right then, one more overworked guy who hadn't slept in days. He didn't have to be Corporal John Crease.

The Coopers' doorbell played an eight-note tune, like an organ in a church. Larry opened the door, dressed in faded jeans and a soil-coloured Parks Canada T-shirt. He was shorter than my old man and softer but they both wore those tintable glasses that grow dark beneath the light of day.

—John, he said.

—Hey, Larry.

They shook hands and Larry ushered us inside. Mitch and his brother, Paul, sat at the table. Paul was a year and a half younger than Mitch but otherwise the same. He had a rounder face, stood inches shorter, smiled perpetually.

Throughout our childhood, Larry would host hotdog cookouts, and in those brittle summers a prepubescent Paul chased neighbourhood girls with grasshoppers and grubs and earthworms he'd dangle like a set of keys. My old man figured he and Paul were equally suave with women.

Larry's wife, Karen, darted around the kitchen multi-tasking like no one I had ever seen. She wore a denim skirt and a knitted beige sweater with the sleeves rolled up. Flour coated her arms to the elbows. When she saw my old man she gave him a big hug that dusted him with white, but her smile said she didn't care one bit. —Oh goodness John it's good to see you.

The house smelled like steak and potatoes. Karen mixed a punch of cranberry juice and ginger ale, and between peeking into the oven and peeking into the barbecue and wiping her hands on a dish towel, she managed to fill six glasses and not burn a thing. My old man offered to help and was told to sit right down. One of Mitch's sisters, Ash, joined us – a redhead one year our junior who I sort of had a crush on. She sat across from me, greeted my old man, and pressed her lips to what could've been a smile.

—Hey Ash, I said.

—William Crease, she said, and I watched her freckles and Mitch watched me with his knowing brotherly eyes.

Before we ate, Larry cupped his hands for grace. —Thank you Lord for the food on the table and the company we share it with, and thank you for bringing John back safely, he's as much a part of this family as anyone seated here today.

The whole dinner, my old man regaled us with stories, mostly about his landlady, a grandmotherly type. They couldn't communicate easily, but she would visit him in the basement with a tray of tea and say —*Chai? Chai?* and he would bring her potato chips from Camp Bondsteel because she loved potato chips. He told us about the times he would come off cadet training so stiff even his heartbeat made him ache. At work, he taught Kosovo police recruits how to fight and how to win; that made him a peacekeeper but not the gunslinging type. His roommate was a Dutchman named Lou who had eight daughters and three ex-wives. The two of them warmed Chef Boyardee in tins and shared candlelight dinners and some nights my old man would find Lou at the table with his food untouched and say, —You waited for me, and Lou would say, —For you, Johnny, I'd wait forever.

Halfway through the meal, cheek full of potato, Larry levelled his fork at my old man and said, —So, how long until you can work again?

—A lesser man would take six months' leave, my old man said.

Larry slurped his punch and mumbled *yup* into the glass.

—Heard you're having trouble with the locals, my old man said.

—Some of the neighbours.

—They egged my truck, Paul said.

—And the upper windows too, Karen said. She laid

her palms flat on the table, thumbs overlapped. —Larry's getting too old to climb out there, especially in winter.

—Might find you elbows-first in the snowbank, eh Lar? my old man said, and Larry loosed a belly laugh and Karen clapped his forearm. My old man gulped a mouthful of punch, considered the tumbler in his big hand, swirled the maroon dregs at the glass's base. —I'll talk to the boys at the office.

Dinner wound on. Larry donned his coonskin hat and when Karen noticed she threatened him with an upheld fork. My old man declined seconds, patted his well-earned paunch. Ash let their dog inside – a great golden retriever who padded to my old man and put its snout in his palm. Mitch snapped photographs with a dispos-able camera and Paul walloped him on the shoulder, and nobody batted an eye. Christ, an ape could have come swinging in on the chandelier and none of us would've cared – we'd known each other that long. It felt like a pocket of childhood, an evening we would all look back upon fondly. Then Larry suggested we head outside to their toboggan hill.

We piled out the entryway, the lot of us. Mitch tugged on a tuque and Ash stepped into snowpants and me and my old man shared a look that said, —Why the hell not? Larry wore his coonskin hat, like always, and hooked his thumbs in his belt and surveyed the flock. Karen was dressed in a puffy spaceman's coat, arms crossed and her eyebrows bent in a show of motherly say-so. On the way around the house, Mitch and Larry each grabbed an oldschool toboggan. They were hand-built, heavy as lumber. Larry called them his snow canoes.

The far edge of their backyard dipped to the gully – the gateway to the wilderness that surrounds Invermere. The glow from the porch teased the outlines of felled trees, frozen chaff scattered along the descent, and clefts in the snow where the Coopers had tested the mettle of their sleds. Mitch planted his toboggan in one of those clefts, grabbed the reins, and looked around for someone to join him. Paul did so, and Larry too – climbed in behind his sons and cracked a joke about three men in a tub. And down they went, one or both of the boys, and maybe even Larry, hooting at the darkness.

—I am in no condition to attempt this, my old man said. The clamber of a crash landing thudded up the hill, the gonging laughter of boys.

—Only a lesser man would go chicken, I said.

—A lesser man would also beat that lippiness out of you.

—Anytime you're ready, old man.

—Just wait boy, he said. —Just you wait.

Ash and Karen boarded the second sled. —Not too fast, Karen said. —My foot is on the brake, Ash told her, and as they teetered on the verge of descent Karen grabbed her daughter at the waist, pressed her cheek to the space between Ash's shoulder blades. They plunged, and I traced their journey and my old man gave me a sudden, one-handed shove. —Women, he said, low enough so none of the Coopers would hear.

Mitch returned, Paul in tow. Snow dusted their cheeks and ice clung to the wool of their tuques. —You guys want a go?

My old man touched his chest. —Best not.

Ash emerged from the darkness. She barely stood to Mitch's shoulders, even though he'd sunk inches into the snow. She belted him a friendly kidney shot and he scowled down at her. Then she and Mitch and Paul boarded one sled while Larry and Karen boarded the other. —A race, Larry hollered, and shoved his kids sideways before speeding off.

The gully swallowed them. —One run, I said to my old man.

—I can't, son.

—You're chickening out.

—You heard what I said.

—Real men –

—*Will*, he said, and my mouth clicked shut. Once, in my younger days, my old man popped both shoulders from their sockets, but even while injured he had not hesitated to wrestle me for control of the living room couch. Downslope, the Coopers took shape in the darkness, as if they were being formed as they ascended. Larry held Paul in a headlock. Mitch had come into possession of the coonskin hat. Ash kept pushing Karen to the snow. The whole time, their laughter rollicked uphill and I thought: here, this is a family.

When I turned to my old man I found him with one arm bent to his chest, clenching a wad of fabric about level with his heart. For a terrifying moment I thought he was having a heart attack, but he must've realized this, because he let go and forced himself straight.

Larry beat me to it, even that far away: —You okay, John?

—It's nothing.

Larry released his son. —Let's head inside.

—It's nothing, my old man called down. Clouds of breath billowed before him. —An ache.

—Dad, I said.

He waved his hand at me, as if to shoo a fly. —Why don't you take a ride with one of them, he said. His voice had lost its roughness and he drawled, low and soft, like he was speaking to alleviate a great suffering. At the time I thought it had to be his injury, that he was in pain, but it's been years and there have been times when he's used that drawl without a wound to speak of. It's the voice he uses when he has to testify against a nephew charged with manslaughter, when he has to bury a sister, when, after decades, he still can't hold a relationship. It's his lonely voice. —Go with Mitchell, or Ashley, he said again. —I don't want you getting miserable on my behalf.

—I'm not sure this counts as getting miserable.

My old man's teeth came together. —Just once, Will. Do what I say?

Right then I'd have dug in my heels, except Ash put her fingers on my arm and derailed my stubbornness, and before I could recover it my old man turned away. Then, almost without knowing it or knowing what I was doing, I lowered myself behind Ash on the sled, and she told me to hang on tight, William Crease, and I looped my arms around her ribs and pressed my chin to her coat. And as wind battered my cheeks and the smell of Ash's wintery hair tickled my nostrils, I imagined my old man behind me, on the slope with arms crossed, dwindling to an outline, a silhouette, a shadow.

AFTERWARD, KAREN BREWED hot chocolate and Mitch changed into a pair of old sweatpants that hung over his feet and made him look like a kid from one of those family movies. Paul asked for marshmallows and Karen told him no. Ash disappeared upstairs. My old man accepted his mug and held it on one palm, suspended under his face so its steam ricocheted off his jaw. —I think I might call it, he said.

    —Let me drive you home, Larry said.

    —I'll hike.

    —It's no trouble, Larry said.

    —I can go on my own.

    —Take a tuque, at least.

    —You drive a hard bargain, my old man said.

    I stayed some time after my old man had pulled a Rough Riders tuque over his ears and ventured into the winter dark. Larry and Karen and Paul and the dog dispersed to the far corners of their house, and Mitch and I moved to the living room. There, he poked at a small fire, gave it a breath of life. A hot chocolate line moustached his lip, but I was a good friend, so I told him about it.

    —I'm worried about my dad, I said.

Mitch cupped his hands on the mug, gave a deep, sagacious nod. Tilt a coonskin hat over his nose and he'd be a spitting image of Larry. —Remember when my dad got lost up in the Hoodoos? he said. —The fall broke something in his back. It took two and a half days to find him. He says all he could do was lie there and pray.

—My dad's not the praying type, I said.

—That's not the point.

—It's not like he hasn't been injured before.

—He never got shot.

—There's no difference, I said.

Mitch swirled the grounds of his hot chocolate and swallowed one last gulp. The fire cackled. —It's like it's inevitable, Will. Since he's a cop, you know? And also it's not inevitable, because this is Invermere, so I bet he always pretended it wouldn't happen, because he had to. Same as dying – you never look it in the eye. But now your dad has to look it in the eye.

On the walk home I smelled snow and street salt and I thought of Ash, my cheek against the spine of her winter coat and my arms that circled her, the superficial fact of our descent. And I thought of the speechless climb and the way I stepped only in the footprints she made in the snow, same as I would have if it'd been my old man who I trudged behind.

HOURS LATER, I woke to the creak of floor joists. A chain rattled. My old man was at the punching bag again, bare fisted, teeth clenched and his glasses off and his attacks savage. He wore a flimsy muscle shirt, and the skin around his collar showed blue with bruising. His punches had lost their finesse and he swung wildly, hick-style, wide haymakers and jabs that started at his shoulder like a hockey fighter. He had his jaw fixed, his head tilted low so his stubble made a dark line along his cheeks. Around his neck he wore a chain with a misshaped hunk of lead on its end, and it bounced and whipped as his fists thrashed the bag. There was a pink smear on the canvas where he'd torn his knuckles. There was a pink dot on his shirt, inches below his left pectoral. His ribs hurt, I bet. A lesser man wouldn't have strapped on the gloves, he'd say. I could see the rise and fall of his breathing: short, gulping – he would confess, later, that it had taken months to build the courage to try a full inhale. Then he fanned one right hook and the punching bag smacked him in the chest, and he staggered a full three steps.

Sweat formed on his bald temples. A line channelled down his cheek, along his neck and collar, and disappeared beneath the shirt to gather, teasing, at the injury he wouldn't let anyone see. The bag lurched, seesawed. My old man studied it, appraised it, wet his lips. Then he brought his fists up and stepped right back in, and I realized, I think, what it meant to be the son of John Crease.

I watched for a long time from the darkness. You don't often see people as they are when nobody else is around. The bag lurched and my old man dodged left, dipped right, followed with a jab and an uppercut, struck with his elbow like he would while inside an opponent's reach.

He'd regained his technique, as though that hint of opposition was enough to remind him how he won his fights. I crept back to my room and listened to the muted beats of fists on canvas and the shifting of his feet on concrete and the occasional dry breath that scraped from his mouth between swings, until at last my old man had worked himself to fatigue and the punching bag's momentum wore itself spent on the chain.

BIG BITCHIN' COW

Biff liked the smell of a truck, the gas and muddy dashboard and the steering wheel smeared with sweat and dirt – manure gone dry, and rust, rust, rust, from bled animals and oxidizing steel and that time he and the boy took one helluva shit-stomping in front of Invermere's only bar. That was because some bonehead in a John Deere trucker cap pawed the boy's girlfriend – woman troubles, always woman trouble with the boy – and until that night Biff had never actually been clubbed with a barstool. Afterward, he and the boy sat in his ratbag Ranger, just bleeding in each other's company, just one ugly pair, cheeks blueing like cabbage head and nicks and burrs up and down their chins. Their eyebrows: split. Their teeth: slick with blood and snot and not all of it their own. —Thanks, Dad, the boy said, and Biff dragged a flannel sleeve over his gums and reached across to pat his son on the knee.

Now, twenty-five years later, that pat was as close to a plan as Biff had, as he drove over the frozen lake in the thunder-cracking hours of the morning. Far off on the horizon the rising sun made the Rocky Mountains glow red and orange like a kerosene lamp. His granddaughter had explained the situation over the phone: the boy discovered a truth about his wife Biff had suspected for years, and then he'd gone hauling-ass to his truck, and then tear-assing down the driveway and around the bend and to the lake. Forty-four years old, the boy, but age doesn't guard against everything – that one Biff knew by heart.

Biff's plan: track the boy across the frozen lake, across all B.C., across the whole of the Great White North if that's what it took, and pat him on the knee. He owed the boy that much and a lot more; nobody else had ever stepped up to save Biff's life. That was on a Prairie farm, the boy no more than thirteen. Not that Biff hadn't almost been killed other than that once – nearly drowned in the Kicking Horse, got real bad pneumonia when he was eleven – but nobody but the boy had ever gone and thrown themselves in front of the raging bull, or however the saying went.

Biff checked the speedometer: one-thirty-eight, on sheer ice. At that speed he'd blast through anything – bullet-through-concrete theory, the boy called it. In the past, he'd mowed down his share of deer and elk and, once, a moose calf at Sicamous near the pulp mill that stunk up the world like propane. He always stopped to double-check he'd killed the animal – didn't like to see things in pain, even bugs – and kept a 30-30 locked in the toolbox behind the cab, in case he hadn't. The only time he didn't slow was when he clipped a black bear, since it was a goddamned bear – a beast designed to crush men's skulls.

As a teenager, the boy, too, had wrecked a few trucks, though not once by hitting an animal. When the boy trashed something it was the good old-fashioned nose-to-ditch style, or passenger-door-to-tree style, or track-jump-followed-by-fishtail-into-city-bench style. Biff had about zero tolerance for idiot driving if it resulted in steeper auto insurance, but the boy got better. He went on to win a couple drag races at the gravel pits, to blitz from the cops one night after a licence suspension, and now, now, how-many-years-later, to cowboy onto the frozen lake and leave Biff chasing tail lights. The boy had a head start and if he reached the far side before Biff caught up then he could disappear into the wilds for good. That scared Biff more than physical violence. That scared Biff more than lizards, and not much did. Without the boy Biff would be one more ass-hapless guy bleating around construction zones – no money, no family, nowhere to go except the cold sucking earth. Biff Crane: a man with nothing to lose. Biff Crane: a man with something to get back, maybe.

Driving on the lake, in the dark, was like driving under-water. He had a globe of light from his highbeams and he could only track his motion by the ice grain slithering beneath his wheels. It felt like floating. It felt like not moving at all. The last time he'd driven on the lake had been with the boy and the boy's wife, them two riding a pair of GTs hitched to his trailer tow. The game: go like a maniac and bank a sharp turn, skid into yaw and slingshot the lovey-dovey brats in an arc. That marked the first time Biff ever locked antlers with the boy's wife, since the boy skidded too near a warm spot and sunk waist-deep in the water. Biff hauled him out – the GT was lost – and packed him into the truck. The boy peeled off his snowpants and sweatpants and, yes, his underpants, and they sat in the Ranger, heat blazing, with the boy's wife between them and everybody's knees brushing everybody's knees. Biff grinned like a stupid man and he could tell the boy was doing his damnedest not to.

—You're an irresponsible bastard, the boy's wife said as they drove to shore.

—That's a good distance from the truth, Biff said, and the boy, naked below the waist but otherwise dressed like a logger, snorted at the window.

The boy's wife was a Calgary cowgirl he met during his first year of electrical school, with dishwater-blond hair and a black cowboy hat she'd only wear when driving her car. She had soft cheekbones and a boyish jawline and a chickenpox scar under her nose. She wore skirts too short to make Biff comfortable. She had a math degree, of all things, and about nobody Biff ever met was as smart as her, and she made a point of it. They were a good match, her and the boy, Biff used to think – even if she voted for the Liberals.

—He could've died, the boy's wife said.

—Well, princess, Biff told her, —you coulda pulled him out yourself.

Biff figured the boy would've snorted again, but his wife jabbed him with her elbow. She wasn't a bad woman, but she could drive Biff into a frenzy with all her left-wing opinions. He held his tongue for the boy's sake: you didn't need to be very smart to call a spayed horse spayed.

That incident would've been a decade ago, and here he was still thinking of it. Mostly, he feared he'd done something wrong, that he should've given the boy some kind of father-son talk. Biff knew about all kinds of fighting, ask anyone, but when it came to matters between a guy and his wife, well, he had only a slate of losses to show. If he could do it again he'd probably do things different, try a bit harder not to get divorced. He never expected he'd die old and lonely. But he bet nobody ever expected that.

The sky was turning turquoise. Biff thought he could see tail lights, but it could have been a reflection, or nothing. He cracked his window a finger to let the morning air enter the cab. He liked the smell of the bleeding hours, the frost or dew and, at home, the scent of a cold house and the cheap, cheap, stovetop coffee he'd strain into a cheap steel thermos and drink in the shower, and while pissing, and while shuffling outside in his Carhartts and steeltoes to let the Ranger's engine wind up in the dry B.C. cold. He didn't envy those poor bastards on the Prairies, like his old man and his two brothers and the stew of fuckers from his ex's side. Romanians – and hillbilly, even by his standards.

Not that he held anything against the ex, really. They got on well enough. She invited him over for holiday dinners, and if he saw her at the bar he'd buy her a drink. One time he helped her chop a cord of firewood and haul it to her backyard in wheelbarrows. He got a peck on the cheek for that, an affectionate rub on the chest. They'd met on the Prairies, went to the same highschool even if they lived in different villages, but that's how it went with all those ghost towns around Regina: get to highschool, partner up, and bunker down. Biff and the ex, at least, made it to B.C. because the province needed electricians, and Biff was, if nothing else, a good electrician.

As he sped along the ice, the edges of his highbeams caught a fishing hut – squat and made of grey lumber, so weatherbeaten it was almost cured – and he almost tapped the brakes, as if that'd do any good. Every year, at least one of those things got taken out by an idiot in a truck, but nobody'd ever been killed, far as Biff knew. His ex used to like fishing in those huts, and he tagged along even though he never saw the charm. You gotta do things like that, Biff figured. You just gotta.

A tough woman, his ex – a denim wearer, coat and all, and the kind of girl who looked good in a ballcap, who could run her fingers through her hair and make you watch. She always had a smudge of dirt or sawdust or oil on her cheek, sure as makeup. She was damn near as strong as him, and if he'd ever had to fight her he wouldn't have wagered either way. One time, when the boy couldn't have been more than ten, Biff and the ex hauled a cargo of teenagers around town so they could hawk Ice-Melt tickets to raise money for their football team. Biff bought a dozen himself, bet on March twenty-second, and when the twenty-second rolled around he and the ex woke in the smoky hours when the Rocky Mountains cast long shadows over town. She smelled like wax paper and bronze, as though she'd been counting change all day, and as he watched her sitting wide-legged in passenger he had a feeling in his gut that the two of them were too similar to last. The ice on the lake had melted, so they were two hundred bucks richer, but rather than celebrate they sat in the Ranger just looking at the view – the glass-work lake lit by the morning sun, as if on fire, as if made of miles and miles of fire. Between them: his cheap steel thermos, her cigarettes. Between them: the gearshift, the empty seat.

Two years later they were divorced. That same summer, Biff and the boy drove eighteen hours to the Prairies and stayed with his brother, Bill, on a cattle farm outside Regina, where Biff drank more home-brewed wine than a man should and where the boy spent whole days in Bill's yard with Bill's dogs – two big Rottweilers named Moose I and Moose II. Biff's clothes were a wreck of torn work tops and khaki pants, and he'd quit shaving. The way his brother stared at him – it felt like coming home beaten. It felt like not coming home at all.

—You still got Princess? Biff said at dinner one day.

His brother nodded – one deep, deliberate dip of his chin. —She had a calf.

—No way.

—After all these years, his brother said.

—She a cow of yours? the boy said through a mouthful of steak.

Biff sucked on his teeth, saw his brother watching. He shrug-a-lugged. —Not only that, he told the boy. —She's my first cow ever. Might not mind seeing her, actually.

—She had a calf, got all mean.

—It's Princess.

—Yeah. But like I say, she's mean now.

Biff barely heard him, took the boy and hopped in the Ranger and made his way to the barn. Then he was facing Princess, his darling cow, who, as a young man, Biff had saved from certain death – the only living creature he could say that for. That time, Princess was pregnant, and Biff woke in the night with this sudden feeling – the same feeling he'd later have about him and his wife, how doomed they were – as if she needed his help. He bolted out the door, ignored his hollering old man, and found Princess in labour. They lost the calf – and every other one, every other time – but Princess persisted.

And now her little sucker of a calf was sucking milk, legs as wobbly as a TV stand. Princess had a bottle-shaped blotch along her bottom ribs. One eye was grey and the other green, and both of them a tad too close together. Her head was big for the rest of her, which itself was pretty damned big.

The boy stayed outside the stall, but Biff went in. Princess's tail whipped against her sides. The bleary-eyed calf slunk toward Princess's hind legs but Biff lowered his palm at it and it seemed to calm. He laid his hand on

Princess's flank – he loved that cow, would've nicknamed his daughter the same had he had one, and never told her its origins.

—Hey, gal, he said.

Princess made a deep, mewling sound in her throat, like a drill stuck in low gear. He patted her, like you might a dog. —Remember me? he said, and she raised her head as if acknowledging that she did, in fact, remember him.

—See? Biff said, turning to the boy.

In hindsight, his warning might have been the scuffing of the calf's hooves on the floor, or the sound of straw kicked into, and then drifting from, the air – like a person flicking dirt off their fingertips. But it happened too fast – too fast, even as he registered something like horror on the boy's face, but not quite horror, because what kind of man gets scared of a cow?

The beast knocked him over with one great bullheaded blow to his blind side. It was like getting blasted through concrete. It was like being pushed underwater – that disorienting. Biff hit the ground mouth first and the muscle above his shoulder – the big one, tough as trailer-hitch, that holds the arm in place and can tow a flatbed – tore nearly in two, and then Princess was on top him, front legs bent to pin him beneath her weight and her big head clubbing him like a madman with a barstool.

Even with two functioning arms he wouldn't have fended her off. His left hung useless, four inches lower than it ought, numb with ache through to his fingertips. He barely knew where he was. He barely knew which way was up. Princess reared her head around, bludgeoning him, but Biff managed on each swing to get his good arm between her head and his. He cracked her in the gums with his elbow. He pushed his thumb into her eye. In his mouth: dirt and cow shit and bits of chewed straw. In his mouth: the rusty, loose-change flavour of his own blood.

Then the boy came. Not thirteen years old, meatless head to toe and in a pair of gumboots and baggy Carhartts belonging to Biff and a stained T-shirt that said: *4U2NV*. He hit the cow like you'd hit a cow to tip one. He put his whole body in the act, shoulder first, toes in the mud, and a face screwed upward and inward with the effort of his heave. He made a sound like a kid would make to help his dad push a truck from the ditch. And Princess barely moved. Sixteen hundred, maybe eighteen hundred pounds, that Princess – one big bitchin' cow. She rocked. Maybe she got distracted. It gave Biff his chance. He stretched his good hand behind his head, to the underside of the wooden stalls, and in a feat of strength he would never repeat, dragged himself from beneath the cow, beneath the stall, and to safety.

The boy vaulted out the moment Biff cleared, and then they limped from the barn and the boy drove the Ranger, since Biff couldn't operate a gearshift. His arm hurt like nothing in the world – worse than the time he got blood poisoning from a wood splinter in the palm, after being flung from the sidecar of his ex-wife's Harley – but he couldn't keep a straight face. The boy gave him this look – a frown damned near comical it was so serious. He held it, sternly, at least for a second. Then the two of them laughed great whooping laughs that shot rings of pain through Biff's shoulder.

—You owe me one, the boy said.

—I sure do, Biff told him.

—You see that – saved your life, the boy said, and he flashed Biff a ridiculous thumbs-up, like you'd give to a guy about to go get laid.

Now, on the frozen lake, Biff would pay the boy back, because he had to, because the boy had saved him from certain death, because nobody gave him the time of day like the boy did, and because there was nothing else in the world Biff cared about more. Everything depended on it – at least, everything that mattered. And as his speedometer cusped one-fifty-seven, the absolute fastest he'd ever got the Ranger moving, he had this sudden gut feeling that he and the boy were in the same driver's seat of the same truck, just two decades separate.

Thirty years ago, thirty years backward in time, while Biff cradled his maimed shoulder and they bounced along his brother's farm road, the boy had grinned a boy's grin that showed all the crooked teeth he wouldn't suffer braces to straighten, and then he reached across the seat and patted Biff on the knee. —It'll all be okay, Dad, the boy said, and Biff, Biff – well, Biff believed him.

DON'T TOUCH THE GROUND

In seventh grade my buddy Mitch Cooper climbed a tree with a handsaw slung over his shoulder on a piece of twine. Later, a kid died. We were only thirteen years old and Mitch needed both hands free so he could shimmy up the trunk. Each time he moved the saw slapped his lumbar. In the hazy light I could see the cotton of his T-shirt translucent from sweat. A red line stained his back from hip to shoulder, but that had nothing to do with the saw. He only looked down at me once, and his left eye was swollen shut and his lip split and he had his teeth bared like an animal enraged.

Earlier that day, I'd met Mitch at the swings outside our classrooms. He had his knapsack one-strapped over his shoulder and both hands in his pockets, was wearing his roughing-it jeans – his oldest pair, patched on the knees and the ass and faded shin to thigh from all the time he spent sliding around in dirt. His arms dangled low and scrawny looking until you grappled them. He liked running, climbing, and building things; by the time he turned nine he had scaled every tree in the neighbourhood

104

except one – a giant pine with no low branches and a trunk so wide even my old man couldn't reach halfway around. Mitch called it the Chevy. I don't know why.

He greeted me with a nod and rubbed his palms together. He smelled like campfires and wood lacquer. It was late May, so his old man would have taken to hotdogs over the firepit and Mitch probably wore the same T-shirt into the smoke the night before. We started our trek home, along the side of the school where Mitch dragged his hand against its stucco.

—I got out early, he said.

—How?

—Mr. Simmons went to the office for something and never came back.

He smiled because he really hated Simmons. I never understood Mitch's hatred, the things he selected.

—I heard his son went blind, I said.

—He just lost an eye.

We passed the tetherball pole and Mitch gave it a running punch. Big signs posted nearby said: *Do not punch the tetherballs.* This was one of the few rebellions Mitch ever dared. The ball swung around and Mitch cocked his arm back for a second hit, but he lacked the coordination. His knuckles grazed the side and the arc bent up like a coat hanger.

—Everyone else is still waiting, he said. —I hate sitting.

—My dad would give me hell, I told him.

His eyebrows tilted like he was mad but they weren't thick enough to be convincing. He came from a religious family, old-fashioned Bible folk, but not the kind that hang pictures of the crucifixion over their toilets. Mitch's old man was a world-famous naturalist named Larry Cooper, which sounds more like a plumber than a bird scholar but there you go. Larry liked looking at photos, talking about birds, and making jokes about boyhood that parents found hilarious. He'd wear big glasses and a coonskin hat, clothes all greys and greens. But he didn't tower like other dads I knew, didn't make you stop and think, *Hey, I'm going to listen to you.* My old man, all two hundred and twenty pounds of him, cold stare and dark glasses, towered. Larry sort of dawdled. He had a retired-cowboy look, would curl one thumb under his belt and give his pants a slow hike. My old man could tell stories about choking out drunks or eating a five-second taser blast or smashing a crook's teeth on the cell bars, and Larry would talk about the time he watched a grizzly bear toboggan down a snowy hill on its ass.

We crossed the playground. Every couple steps Mitch turned to see if anyone was coming. We headed to the gully, a forested area separating the subdivision where we lived from the grade school. A ringwire fence rimmed the playground, and Mitch ran and tried to vault it but didn't quite make the height, and as he descended he took a nasty gash down his back.

He balled up his T-shirt for me to see. —How bad is it? he said.

The scratch spanned from his kidney to his shoulder blades. It was deepest and reddest at the hip. —It's welting, I said.

—Is it gonna get blood on my shirt?

—Maybe.

—Is it?

The scratch looked like someone had drawn a red line across his back with a felt pen. —I don't know, I said.

—If you see it getting stained let me know, alright?

—It's just a T-shirt, I said.

—Yeah, but let me know.

Then a green Ford Ranger screamed by us with teenagers piled in the bed. One of them pointed at Mitch and even though I couldn't hear him over the muffler I knew exactly what he'd said – *fag*, or *jew*, which made no sense but which the hicks used to describe things they hated. The truck braked and U-turned and cars honked at it to no avail.

—Let's go, I said.

The truck eased up beside us and kept our pace as we walked along the street. Rat-faced hicks in the cab snickered and smoked and one of them raised his arm to throw something. The guy in the passenger's side was a kid named Jordan who wore a blue hockey jersey and a ballcap on backward. He could recite any of the speeches from his favourite WWF wrestlers, had a half-finished cigarette tucked behind his ear and a loose grin on his face, as though his cheeks had come unyoked from the jaw.

—Hey, piglet, Jordan said.

My old man had told me to ignore people like him because they'd always be there, because there were guys who truly hated cops and would tell their kids to pick on me, and because if I didn't ignore them then I'd have to live every day by the bone in my knuckles. I'd have kept going without even looking at them, but Mitch – Mitch stopped dead in his tracks. The hicks in the truck hooted; this is what they wanted. I gave Mitch a sharp order to keep going, but he didn't. One of the truck's doors clicked open.

—Leave us alone, Mitch said.

Jordan looked at his buddies in the cab and smiled as if Mitch had made a joke. —Why? he said, and moved his jaw in a chewing motion.

Mitch had nothing to say to that. He eyed me and I motioned with my head that we should go. A car behind the truck laid on its horn and Jordan gave them the finger, turned away for just a moment, and Mitch and I burst into a sprint.

We cut along the road against traffic. Mitch was a good runner but I wasn't. The hicks had pulled over and guys spilled out the doors. They ran at us with wobbly legs. I thought the only hope we had was the gully and Mitch must have thought the same. Jordan and his friends hadn't even covered half the distance when we veered through the ditch and down a path we'd taken home for the last four years.

Behind us, Jordan yelled threats. He'd find us. The gully wasn't that big.

But, well, it was – the gully served as a gateway into the vast, undeveloped wilderness of the Kootenay Valley. Mysteries happened there: hunters claimed to watch animals withstand deer-slugs through the jugular; some teenagers erected a fort where the forest relinquished to beach, and a month later that fort was gone and three girls with it; fires glowed in the distance, always out of sight, and people whispered about the feral things that can never be tamed. Hooligans built rope swings and smashed beer bottles on pine trees but nobody ever found the glass. Boys were broken, body and spirit – claimed by the gully – and people would remember them and cluck their tongues and think, *They could've gone far.*

In the gully truckloads of teenagers didn't threaten to beat us with their bike helmets. In the gully Mitch knew the quickest way anywhere. He pretended to be a great hunter, would kneel before a footprint and run his index along the shape, push his tongue into the corner of his mouth. He'd pick a name he hated, like Ford Helmer, and when I asked him how he knew he'd note the depth of the impression. —Helmer's a big guy, he'd say. —He has heavy feet.

Wherever we went in that gully, Mitch led. We never took the easy way. We'd sneak about on the dirty hillsides and search for others like ourselves and, if the coast was clear, Mitch would skid down to the path on the heels of his sneakers. There, he reached for low-hanging branches and coiled them down to hook onto roots – if a kid came by, those branches would whip them in the teeth. At least that was the plan. But each day the branches were unhitched and swaying like power lines, and I dare you to tell Mitch the wind had blown them free. It was other kids. Getting hit in the teeth.

The gully was just practice for him, small change. As an adult, he'd ward off a cougar with one-liners from *Dirty*

Harry and a pair of sticks held akimbo. He once lost three thousand dollars of camera equipment down a chasm on Jumbo Glacier; he fought a bear, at a cabin in Dunbar – scurried onto the roof and when the beast clambered after him he bludgeoned it with the chimney bucket.

But he was one hell of a woodsman even that day in grade seven. We moved with extra caution because we figured Jordan and his friends would be back. You never really defeat the hicks. Not in that town. Not at that age. They had nothing better to do. They were unavoidable, like chicken pox, and they never lost a fight because even if you knocked one down they'd just lie to their friends.

Mitch crouched low amid the foliage. His T-shirt was muddied and dirty and I didn't tell him this but the blood from his back had soaked through. He picked at a nearby bush and snapped its branches as he sat.

—Think we lost them? he said.

—It's quiet.

He bit the corner of his lip. There were more than a dozen places where we could have climbed out of the gully, could have got off scratch free.

—Think they'll be watching the entire road? he said.

—They have better things to do.

Mitch didn't answer. He picked at that bush and snapped the twigs and tossed them one by one onto the ground, squinted his eyes. I sat and waited for him to finish thinking. I could see schemes whirring in his mind, the way his forehead pulled in, the way he played with a twirl of his brown hair. He didn't get to rebel much.

—I bet they're watching the road, he said.

—Maybe.

—Are you scared?

—No.

—Let's go check the rope swing, he said.

—Why?

—In case they're there. So we know not to go that way.

—They'll beat us up.

—I'll take a stick, he said, and wandered a small distance on his knees and hefted a stick from the ground. It was long and a little green and not brittle. A good stick.

—Are you scared? he said.

—No.

Mitch could have cut circles around those guys, even if they were at the rope swing. He could have picked any number of ways to get home. Even back then I knew this, but I had an idea why Mitch was dragging out this chase. Once, when we were in grade three, Mitch hucked a clump of yellow clay at a group of kids several grades above us. They gave chase immediately but we evaded them by hiding in a hole beneath the natural gas tank in his backyard. He grinned the whole time we spent under that tank, pressed against the warm dirt, the tinny metal above us smelling like a boiler room.

We picked our way through the gully because the hicks might have been on the paths. Mitch lifted branches out of his way and eased them back so they wouldn't smack me in the face. Every time a twig broke beneath him, every time a branch held its sway too long, I expected Jordan or one of his friends to burst from the trees and drag us away by our hair.

The rope swing hung in the gully pretty much halfway between Mitch's house and the school. It dangled from a tree and was visible from the road, but only if you knew where to stand and where to look. Over the years, kids' hands had frayed the thing from cinch to tip. It had knots along its length like fists. Mitch could climb the entire thing and then shimmy down the tree trunk, but, back then, I didn't have the strength to get more than a quarter of the way up.

As we neared the rope swing I heard the sound of a bottle breaking and froze. Mitch went motionless mid-step and cocked his head. It would take me years to realize just how good Mitch was at that moment; where I had heard the sound of breaking glass, he heard something else. Footsteps, maybe. Wood snapping. A heavy, unnatural breath out of sight. He looked back at me and he seemed to have aged. His fingers furled and unfurled around the stick. His lips moved like he was counting.

Then he took off.

One of the hicks bolted from the trees nearby. He chased after Mitch and gave a yell. Voices joined him, feral sounds like dogs that divide the world into things they can kill and things they can't. I stayed hidden, chest flat against the earth and the smell of dirt and bugs so close I could taste them. It seemed like it took forever for them to catch Mitch.

When I heard them laugh, a ways off, I dared move enough to peer at the rope swing. They had Mitch inside a circle. He held his stick like a quarterstaff, in front of him. Jordan was inside the circle too. Mitch would be able to smell him, the cigarettes and booze and the muskiness a kid gets when he hasn't showered in days – a scent as though he'd been sitting in front of a fire and someone had pissed in it.

The hicks passed around a beer and someone lit a cigarette. Jordan peered over his shoulder at them with a grin on his face like an ape. He faced Mitch again and offered the beer in his hand. Mitch leaned away from it and his nose curled up.

—Want to get drunk? Jordan said. He had his hand around the bottleneck, the mouth capped with his thumb, wagging the beer in Mitch's face. He told Mitch religion was stupid and God hated him and that he had stupid pants. He poured a bit of beer on Mitch's head.

—Have a sip.

—No.

—Drink it or I'll take you on a trip down smack-down lane.

His friends chuckled. Mitch turned away and prodded the ground with his stick. I knew Mitch for a long time back then, and I never saw anything on his face like that day in grade seven. He was going to do something stupid but I didn't yell a word of warning, and I still don't know if I should have. Jordan stretched his arm out to pour more beer and Mitch spun around and rammed him in the nuts with the stick. It was lightning-fast. It was a direct hit. Jordan dropped the beer, wheezed a long breath onto the forest floor, and without him having to say anything, the circle closed and I lost sight of Mitch in the throng.

WHEN IT WAS OVER, when they left Mitch on the ground with his hands over his face, when Jordan limped back to his truck with his buddies, I came out from the trees. I went to Mitch and sat down beside him. He sniffled loud and swallowed. I helped him sit up and he leaned against the rope swing's tree. His eye was swelling and his lip was split and he favoured his left side. I brushed dirt off his shoulder, tugged moss from his hair.

—I got him good, Mitch said.

—Yeah.

—Good thing I took that stick.

He dabbed his mouth with the back of his hand. When he saw it was red he curled his lip in and sucked on it. I'd never seen someone actually beat up. My old man once came home bleeding, but it was just his nose. I saw a kid wipe out on a bike and scrape his face along the asphalt. I'd seen it in movies. It's not the same. They never wince like Mitch did. You don't smell the sweat on them, the sourness and the rustiness of their breath. People are not stoic; they do not suffer prettily.

—You could have taken him one on one, I said.

—He's a bit too big, Will.

—Maybe.

Mitch cringed as he stood up. I saw his stick in the distance and brought it over.

—Let's go home, I said.

Mitch held his stick in front of him. He turned it over in his hands and ran his finger across it in a wood-cutting motion. Then he slapped the stick against his palm and shook his head. He told me his plan and I was too stupid to object. First, he'd need a handsaw, which he could get from home, but before going home, he wanted to clean himself up, in case his folks caught him.

We trekked to the beach where he could wash himself in the lake. He kicked off his shoes and socks, rolled his jeans to his knees, and waded into the water. The sun was setting over the Purcell Mountains, out across the lake. Mitch went deep enough for the water to touch the bottom of his kneecap, and then he scooped it against his face and scrubbed away the caked blood and tears.

When he took a sip, I said: —You shouldn't drink it.

—Why?

—Swimmer's itch.

He rubbed his moist fingers against the tender parts of his face. —But I'm thirsty.

—I can go get you some water.

—I'm alright.

—The swelling is going down, I told him.

—It still hurts.

—We can stop by my place if you want.

—No, he said.

He dipped his hand in the lake again, laid his cooled knuckles against his cheek and the bones around his eye that were going blue and purple and shades of yellow-brown. He smacked his lips and they looked cracked and dry as hide. I wish I hadn't told him not to drink the water.

We went to his house. He crept into his garage and swiped a handsaw from his dad's toolbox, as well as two Cokes and a length of twine. I didn't open my Coke in case Mitch wanted it later. He pressed the cold aluminum against his lip for a second, then cracked it. He drank in long, heavy slurps.

It was starting to get dusky by the time we made it back to the rope swing. Mitch handed me his Coke, and then he put the sides of his shoes against the trunk and hugged the tree. He scaled it in inches. Each time he moved it was up, and he looked down only once. I nodded. I had an inkling of what could happen, even then. Mitch hoisted himself onto the branch and pulled the saw around where he could use it.

In less than a day one of Jordan's friends would hop onto the rope and rip the whole thing, branch and all, down atop himself. He'd bang his skull and die on the operating table and the papers would print a photo of the boy cradled in two uniformed arms. I'd see the picture and miss three days of school, and Mitch would walk around like a beaten kid for months. One day after a sleepover my old man would catch my arm and ask, softly, if I knew everything was alright with him, at home.

That branch took Mitch a long time. He didn't have a great position and he got sore fast. It darkened but he was not swayed, just sat on that branch and shifted when he had to. I threw him the other Coke underhand and he plucked it straight from the air. He sawed and sawed and sawed until that branch was cut within half an inch.

After he finished, we walked around the gully for a while. He had a new, gnarled stick in his right hand and the handsaw slung over his shoulder. A woodland creature had hollowed a bowl in the middle of a stump and filled it with debris and I wondered how deep that hole went. The air smelled like paving salt and pine needles and the cadaverous swell of the lake. Saplings as high as my shin jutted from the moist dirt. We didn't say much. Someone's bass thumped in the distance. We were, I hope, too young to understand what could happen.

We walked home. The last light seeped behind the Purcells and the stars appeared. Mitch tried to talk about how awesome the chase was. He pointed at the stars because his class just finished studying the solar system. He said he couldn't quite make them out because of his swollen eye, and then he touched the puffiness on his face, winced. It was all very superficial.

—You alright? I said.

—Yeah.

—Wanna stop at my place first to get cleaned up?

—Your dad will be mad.

—No, I said. —He won't.

Mitch shrugged. He tossed the stick aside. —It's probably too late.

VALLEY ECHO

RATCHET

The boy's mother insisted her son be named Winston, because it evoked hints of rubbled London and because she remembered her old man, a gunned-down naval aviator who she eventually discovered had raped her mother. She announced her decision with one arm bent like a coat hanger behind her head. Conner liked *Winston* about as much as getting bitched at, and he couldn't even shorten it to anything worthwhile: Win, Winny, Winsy. A man called Winsy would shave his armpits and watch foreign movies. Conner's boy should have a tougher name, like Dick or Tim, or even simpler, and with an *r*: Ray, or Ern – a name he could wing pinecones at, a name that could torque a crescent wrench.

For ten hours each day Conner shaped steel pipe with a hydraulic choke while his buddies trawled 500-grade tech cable from great nautical spools. They were doing re-haul on the local sawmill. He toiled alongside a metal-worker named Jack who wore a navy jumpsuit and a tinted mask that left his chin bare to sparks. All shift, the steel ionizing beneath his arc welder smelled like baseboard heaters. Some lunch hours, Jack's twenty-two-year-old wife rolled up in a Rocket 88, cherry red, all that muscle like an athlete. It had chrome accents and leather seats and straps that fastened in an X at a man's solar plexus. Jack's wife parked near the retaining wall where Conner ate jelly sandwiches with the guys. A handsome woman, Jack's wife – blond ringlets teased her collar, lipstick, and this way about her like a reliable set of knockouts. Jack and her would be forty-five minutes, tops. When they returned, he hiked his crotch and Conner eyed his wife and on more than one occasion she eyed him back.

At the end of every week a smudged envelope appeared on top of the pipe threader, Conner's name scrawled along the seal. No paper trail, of course – this was cash for cash's sake. He shuffled the bills into a lockbox he hid in plain sight on his bedroom windowsill beside a small cactus and a burned-out Maglite.

Some weekends he left Winston with a nanny so he and the boy's mother could spend fifty straight hours shitfaced on hash. She dribbled candle wax on her wrist and peeled it off like skin. Conner cruised cooking channels and mimicked master chefs' chopping motions on his leg with the remote. One time they watched a rerun marathon of *The Twilight Zone*, pawing each other's limbs while on the television a mud-soused huntsman Vietnammed his way through the Mississippi wilderness. In those days, before the boy's mother fucked everything up, they could screw and he wouldn't be haunted by her handlebar ribs. He liked to hook his thumb in her mouth. She had shapely gums. He had decent stamina. They'd have separate, unremarkable orgasms.

Then, on a clear day in October when leaves piled the streets, Winston's mother climbed into a two-seater Datsun and took off for Vegas with the lockbox and a pregnant school friend named Eileen. The boy was two. Conner spent one full day so fucked he awoke naked in a hotel room beside Jack's wife. The room smelled like used sheets and latex. It had musky wallpaper and a titty-lamp mounted on the ceiling above the bed. Residual white grains lingered on the nightstand. Her pale back faced him and in the amber light her blond hair looked ruddy and her skin tanned. She was weeping and she shrunk toward her knees when he trailed his knuckles along her spine.

Conner pulled it together. At dawn he'd drop Winston at his old man's acreage at the outskirts of Edgewater. His old man wore flannel shirts and his skin was brown and farmered below the elbow. A scar halved his right ocular and a glass eye lolled in that socket like a ball bearing. When Conner came home he pinged spare change into a Folgers tin he and the old man set aside for a new TV, so they could replace the panelboard relic slouched in a corner. The old man barbecued steaks. He mashed potatoes with barbaric, two-handed thrusts. In the evenings they sipped heavy beer and watched news coverage of the war and lounged on the porch passing the toddler between them. At least once, the old man told Conner he'd done him proud.

After a while the boy's mother showed up penniless and a cokehead. Conner shut the door on her. She threatened to lay abuse charges, showed him finger bruises on the soft flesh beneath her biceps and the bulge of her jugular. He called her a fucking whore. She said it'd be a shame for Winston to see his dad hauled to jail.

A few summers later, while the boy's friends skewered grasshoppers on willow spears, Conner and him hung a tree fort off a pine so thick around the base they couldn't ring it, even with their fingertips touching. Winston's mother had fucked off on another binge with her whore friend Eileen. Conner and the boy fashioned a pulley system around the tree's branches, and as his son helped him heave on a rope to hoist the base, the nickname came to him: Winch.

EVENTUALLY, CONNER SNAGGED his ring finger in a pipe threader and the machine tugged it off with humbling nonchalance. He pressured his maimed hand in an oil rag and traced the wrecked bone beneath the cloth. At the hospital they stitched him but told him there wasn't enough left to reattach. The doctor asked if he wished to keep the remains, maybe in a pickle jar, and then he laughed like a man who'd used that joke before.

The finger healed but he didn't get any money since

he worked under the table. His old man knew a few guys in management at a barium mine forty minutes away. Conner and him spent a night awake until the morning light cleared the mountains. Dirty work, the barium mine, and thankless, and likely to put him out of commission with lung defects in two decades. Upstairs, Winch coughed in his sleep.

—Et'll pay the bills, his dad said, and Conner nodded into his wrist.

Not long after, Conner was braving the rainy highways with one hand knuckled at the twelve-o'clock and one hand on the gearshift. Deer crowded the ditches and one time he swerved to the opposite lane when he rounded a blind curve. His ancient Ford shuddered like a desperate mutt. Cars churned slop onto his windshield. The air blasting through the radiator smelled like woodsmoke and if Conner sucked a deep breath it tickled his nostrils like his dad's cigarettes used to, when he was a kid riding shotgun through the hoarfrost hours of the morning.

A year through the work, he came home and found his dad at the base of his porch with a busted hip. He was propped on an elbow and he leaned his head against the lowest step.

—Cunt took Winch, his dad said.

Inside, Conner dialed the hospital and told them his old man broke a hip. The Folgers tin was on its side and looted except for loose change. He slammed the receiver.

—Go get yer boy, his dad said when Conner knelt to help him inside.

He did. At his home, he found a ratbag Benz 230 parked on the front lawn. Inside the house, Winch hunched on a lemon-coloured sofa with patches of foam torn out like a bloodied creature. The boy looked alright, was toying with a shoe-sized buggy constructed from a scrapped Meccano set.

—Y'awright? Conner said.

Winch nodded.

The boy's mother was in the kitchen.

—Ya can't come in here, she said.

Conner booted a chair out of his way and in two steps had her by the neck. He heaved her at the drywall and it crunched. She clawed his four-finger grip. His old man once told him people change when you've got them where you want them. You can see it, his dad said. Their wild, desperate eyes.

Conner pushed his knuckles upward against her nose so her chin tilted.

—Ya hurt muh dad an' took muh savins, he said.

A throaty sound choked against his palm. He drew his fist back to his ear and watched her track it with her eyes.

—I thought you were gonna hurt muh boy, Conner said.

He dropped her. She landed on her ass in a crumple and made a long, whinnying noise. Conner led Winch to his Dodge Sweptline and they drove to the hospital where his old man was strung up in a cushy bed. In a day's time the house would burn to cinder and he and the boy would toe through the rubble. He got a handful of insurance paid out but houses in Edgewater had little value. They moved to his old man's place officially and Conner spent the cash on a colour TV and a set of winter tires, and on the day his old man hobbled home the three of them crashed on the couch and watched *The Spy Who Came in from the Cold*.

WINDLASS

When Winch turned twelve, him and his dad and his dad's friend Sampson – who his dad called Doc – and Sampson's son, Dallas, packed into a '60 Bronco and tear-assed to a cabin out at Brisco. His dad had taken the weekend off. He worked more and more and sometimes Winch wouldn't see him for days at a time, or he'd shoulder through the front door before bed. Those days, Winch's grandpa – his gramps – rose from the couch and zigzagged to the kitchen to heat food. Winch's dad gamed with the cabbage-like smell of pulp, and rust, and he'd have pink-stained hands from the barium, but Winch liked the way he had scratchy whiskers. His dad would sleuth one eye sideways and he'd pretend not to notice, and his dad would start to growl, and if Winch smiled he'd get tackled and they'd wrestle a few minutes, until his gramps brought a plate and a beer in a giant ceramic mug with a picture of two guys tending a bonfire. —Awright you two, his gramps would say. —Don't make me sepraychya.

Sampson and his truck smelled like mothballs. He had a jean jacket with hewn edges, worn open over a Black Sabbath sweatshirt. His cheeks were narrow and tanned and his nose jabbed forward with a hook. He habitually lifted his Coors Light hat straight off his head so he could swipe a hand over his matted hair. Winch's dad filled the passenger seat in a checkered overcoat and jeans faded in swaths and a beaten blue ballcap. He had the kind of hard cheekbones that could absorb their share of blows, and Winch had seen them bruised and bloodied more than once over the years.

Dallas was a beaver-toothed kid with freckles who talked about rifles all day. Winch had never touched a rifle, but his gramps kept one locked in a fibreglass case above his headboard.

It was September. Rain clouds stirred over the mountaintops and already the peaks had whitened with snow. The morning smelled like winter, the scent of brick and pale sunlight. Winch and his dad flung supplies into the rear of Sampson's canopied Bronco. His dad fished two granola bars from inside a backpack and flicked one over and they chewed on the bars while Sampson spot-checked. Winch's dad mentioned the poor state of his treads and Sampson jerked a thumb toward the box, a milk crate full of chains. —I'm from the Prairies, he said.

While they drove, Sampson smoked cigarettes from a carton he kept in the glove compartment. He lowered his window and flicked ash over the glass and flecks of it whirled back into Dallas's face.

—I saw yer girl, Sampson said.

—She's not muh girl, Winch's dad said.

—Even still.

—Don't care to hear about it.

Sampson crushed his cigarette in a white foam mug taped beneath the radio.

—She's gone and cleaned.

—Ya know where I stand.

—Maybe ya should give 'er a chance.

—Maybe you should keep yer fingers outta this pie, Winch's dad said, and belted Sampson on the shoulder.

They veered off the highway. Sampson's Bronco bobbed over roots and divots and Winch bounced against the restraint. His dad braced one palm against the dashboard and the other clutched the oh-shit handle above the passenger window. Tree branches whipped by, clunked into the windshield and the roof.

—Why we gotta come all the way out here? Winch's dad said.

Sampson seemed to eye Winch's dad sideways. —Et's a big load, Con.

—Seems a long way is all.

—Bein safe. Ya know?

Winch's dad clicked his teeth. —Just seems a long way out.

—That's the point, Con. No one sees nothin.

—Don't like havin muh boy here for it, neither, his dad said, and when he realized Winch was listening he gave a big wink.

They got a few kilometres down the dirt road before a fallen tree blocked the way and Sampson platformed the truck trying to bog over it.

—Fucken truck, he said.

126

Winch's dad dropped the seesawing distance to the ground and dusted his hands together with two brisk swipes. —Lock 'er in four-wheel, he said.

—She ent a four-wheel.

—Sonabitch.

His dad circled the truck and Winch twisted in his seat.

—Put 'er in gear, his dad called, and then he slammed his shoulder against the box and heaved. His boots dug in the damp earth, and when Winch glimpsed his dad's face it was red and bunched together. The truck teetered, its front tires touched down, and then Winch's dad fell away.

—Winch! Get down here and gimme a hand.

—I'm comin Con, Sampson said.

—I said Winch come help. Doc, you stay in yer sissy truck so it don't steer into a tree.

Winch scrambled between the seat and ducked out the door. His dad had his lips pulled in a half grin and he gave Winch a little shove. —Let's get this done, he said, and on a three-count they plowed the tailgate and Winch heaved and his dad's boots dug gruelling progress and the truck skidded forward over the log so the rear tires bit the tree bark. Sampson hooted. Winch's dad hawked and spat and wiped his sleeve along his mouth. —Takes one an' a half men, eh Winch? he said, and winked.

The cabin sagged on one side like a wounded dog. Its exteriors were dark cedar. A tarp and poles jutted off the side and Sampson parked the truck beneath this makeshift carport. He turned the key in the ignition and the truck juddered to sleep. —Here we are, he said, and stretched.

While Sampson took his keys to the door, Winch helped his dad lug four packs from the truck. When he lifted the nearest one, it was heavy and objects swung inside it like bricks. He loosened the strings to peer inside but his dad tore it away from him.

—Don't be a snoop, his dad said.

His dad superheroed three of the four bags and Winch scurried behind with his own. They hucked the packs in a corner except one, which his dad handed over to Sampson with a nod. The rat-faced man slid it into a cupboard and brushed his hands together and let out a breath that puffed his cheeks.

Winch's dad handed him a couple sixers of Kokanee and told him to sink them in the lake. Dallas joined him, a BB gun slung against his shoulder like an army cadet and a grocery bag full of empties dangling from the tip. Winch weighted the sixers with a football-sized rock and staked a branch in the sand so his dad could find the beer, then him and Dallas balanced the empties on bleached driftwood. Dallas pinged coloured bullets off the cans and glass bottles and never offered Winch a go. Sampson hoofed it to the lake's edge and tore two cans free of their yoke and pressed one to his cheek. He gave an affirmative nod, like a man who knew the right temperature for beer, and then climbed to the cabin where Winch's dad reclined on the porch.

—Met yer mum, Dallas said.

—She's a bitch.

—Muh dad likes 'er.

Winch rolled onto his back. Dark clouds rolled over the mountaintops. He looked for the haze that meant rain.

—Last I seen 'er she took a bunch of money.

—Yer dad was mean to 'er.

—Well, yeah, Winch said. —She deserves it.

For lunch they ate game meat pressed into burgers. —Not even the haunch of the six-pointer I got, Sampson said. —Got 'em through both lungs. Shoulda seen the sucker keel.

They wheeled a grouchy propane barbecue from inside and Winch's dad scorched his face when the old thing fireballed. They all laughed. His dad got the barbecue going and it wheezed thin smoke out its sides, and Sampson smacked bloody wads onto the grill with one cupped hand. Winch listened to them sizzle.

—Y'ever seen muh gun? Sampson asked after he'd shut the lid.

Winch's dad pursed his lips and said, —Nup.

—Gimme a sec, he said, and darted inside. He returned with a rifle held before him like a ceremony, a smile big enough to reveal a missing canine. —Three-oh-eight Winchester. Bolt-action.

He ratcheted the bolting mechanism and sighted through the scope, made a *pow* noise and faked a recoil strong enough to blast him backward into a deck chair. Dallas laughed in a slow ribbit: *huuh-huuh-huuh*.

Afterward, they lounged full-bellied in the deck chairs. Sampson and Winch's dad nursed beer and Dallas and him sucked on Cokes. Sampson faced the three of them, not reclined, elbows fanned to the sides on the arm rests like a man who might rise suddenly. He lifted the Coors Light cap and brushed a palm across his matted hair. A couple times he tapped a finger on his gums. The Winchester leaned against the cabin's wall, arm's reach, draw distance.

—Wanna head out on the boat? Sampson said.

—S'a two person, enn'it? Winch's dad said.

—Dally ken steer it. Let the boys have a go.

Winch's dad slurped from his beer, tipped his head and jiggled the can.

Sampson was leaning forward on his knees. —What'dya think, Dal?

Dallas mumbled to his chest.

—Didn't raise ya to be a chickenshit, Sampson said.

—Can go with our boys, Winch's dad said. —Take a turn. Might not mind a go muhself.

Sampson pitched his empty sideways along the porch. —Pfah, he said, then spat. —Least yer boy ent too chicken-shit to go out. He stood and wrapped one greasy palm around the Winchester's barrel and caught Dallas by the collar. The two of them lurched to the lake's edge.

Winch's dad was half on his feet. Sampson planted the rifle in the sand and it fell over instantly. Waves lapped its heel. He had Dallas by the shirt and he swung his gaze from his son to the rifle. Then he smacked the boy with his free hand, just the fingers, but hard enough for Dallas to clench his teeth, squinch his eyes.

—What kinda feet per second this thing get, Doc? Winch's dad said, coming down the beach.

Sampson swayed sideways and released his son. He lifted the rifle in two hands and held it waist level like a gangster. —Fuck ef I know, he said, and blinked heavily. —Let's get the boys on the water, let 'em have some fun.

Winch's dad closed his fist around the Winchester's barrel. —Might be ya had enough to drink, Doc, he said.

Sampson tugged. —Fuck off.

—I'll just go put 'er back.

Sampson tugged harder. Winch's dad stepped forward heavily, didn't release. —Don't be an idiot, he said.

—Ricki said you were a dick, ya know.

—*Fuck. Her*, Winch's dad said.

—We're a pair now.

—Doc, let go of the gun.

—Fuck you Conner et's *my* gun.

His face was scoured inward but all at once it went lax, his lips drooped, eyes unsquinched. He smiled. —Eh, look at us. Let's just get the boys on the water an' forget about all this.

Winch and his dad shared a look. His dad's jaw went stiff but his eyes sagged and Winch understood he ought to take Dallas out, to get Sampson to shut up, distract him. —Come on Dal, he said.

Sampson kept his tin boat some ways down the shore, anchored to a felled tree with a carved-up trunk. The boat had a plastic bench from port to starboard and a rusted-out motor with a pull-cable so stiff and knotted

Winch could barely wiggle it. Behind them, his dad and Sampson stood off, too far for Winch to hear them talk. Occasionally, one would tug and the other would shake his head. Dallas untethered the boat and passed Winch a gnarled paddle and they pushed off and the underside scraped the lake bottom.

They paddled across the water, not out on the water but toward their dads, a shallow arc. The sun lit the lake's surface like a grease fire. Both men had changed positions: his dad had his back to the water now, shoulders rolled down and head hunched and fists at his side. Sampson had the .308 levelled at his dad's chest. From that range it'd blow a man's heart clear out. As Winch and Dallas paddled nearer, their voices skipped across the water, mere murmurs at first.

—Pretty dummuya, Winch's dad was saying.

—Don't have a choice. She said ya got a bunch of loose cash.

—Gave that up. She robbed me twice.

The boat rocked suddenly and Winch tore his eyes from the shore to see Dallas terror-gripped on the boat's edge. He was throwing his weight back and forth and his eyes were pinched shut and he made a humming noise.

—Dal, stop, Winch said.

—I don't like boats, he said.

Water sloshed over the tin edge and soaked his shoe. Winch tried to throw his weight counter to Dallas but it didn't seem to matter. The boat seesawed in the water, tottered, and splashed aright. Winch grabbed for the other boy, tried to hold him steady, but Dallas had fear-strength and he was muttering to himself. Water sloshed over the gunwales. The hull rocked.

—Dal! Winch said.

—I don't like boats, Winch.

—Our boys are goin under, Winch heard his dad say.

—Ya gotta do it, Sampson said. —Ya gotta.

—Nope. Nope Doc.

—Y'owe me, Con man, y'owe me.

—I don't owe ya. I'm here aren't I. Wer square.

—Wer not square, Con man.

Winch gulped a mouthful of air as Dallas stood up and the boat flipped. He hit the water cheek first and the shock of the chill nearly drew the breath from his lungs. The boat beat his calves as it overturned and Winch propellered around until he could stop himself. The boat's base cut the lake's oil-lamp surface. They weren't far from the shore but no one had ever taught him to swim. He kicked out. He raked his hands through the water. His shoes weighted his feet and his clothes shucked against his skin. That gulp of air hung in his throat, right at the soft divot above his breastbone, and already he felt pressure building. Sunlight pierced the darkness under the water. Sediment and tackle-like debris lit up like stars.

He found himself in a sphere of light as though in a candlelit room. His gums shrunk inward with the cold. His eyes stung. He swished water in his mouth and tasted seaweed, clamminess, the eel-like texture of his inner cheek. At the cusp of his vision a weatherbeaten truck rusted at the bottom of the lake. Algae eked along its sagging tires and the exposed metal under paint. Corrosion had eaten the hood, and the engine and all its parts sparkled when the water's surface shifted. The driver door faced him, loose on its hinges, as though the man behind the wheel had bailed in a hurry. Winch knew stories about guys who lost their trucks to the frozen water. The side said: *Chevrolet*. It was like no Chev he knew anyone to drive. Old. It had to be old. He once saw a burnished-bronze truck trundle into a parking space between two baby pines, on the main street, outside the candy shop, and as the engine wound down it had stuttered, violently, and backfired a clot of exhaust with a loud *KA-BLAM*, muffled thunder, deep but loud enough for Winch, suspended under the water, to hear and wonder at.

Then he was rushing upward and air whispered on his cheek and then mud sucked at his hair. His dad towered above him, ballcap gone, damp hair combed over the crest of his skull, his jeans and checkered shirt watersopped and heavy. Winch coughed and spewed lake water and pushed onto his elbows. His dad had one arm pressed to his side and his lips peeled over his teeth and his greying hair matted to his head. Blood smeared his open hand and the flannel overcoat where his arm snugged fabric to torso.

—Y'awright? Winch heard himself say.

His dad nodded. —Ya need a minute?

—Throat hurts.

Winch got to his feet and tucked his shoulder under his dad's armpit and his dad let weight onto him. Sampson was spreadeagled on the shore. Waves licked the soles of his steeltoes. Dallas shivered beside him.

—Get the keys, Winch's dad said, and Winch eased from beneath the arm and his dad tilted sideways, winced. Dallas kept still as Winch rifled through Sampson's pockets. A *Go Flames* dog tag dangled from the key chain. The .308 lay half-submerged, waterlogged, spent.

—Get the gun too, his dad said.

Winch fetched it, felt the weight in his hands like a baseball bat.

—Might need you to drive, his dad said.

—Is he dead? Dallas said, and tapped Sampson on the chest.

—Choked out. He'll live. Get inside where it's warm.

Winch drove his dad to the hospital. The doctors phoned his gramps and the old guy showed up without the fake eye. He clutched the hem of his checkered coat. Those big hands were bone-white and the empty socket, rinsed and wet with saline, glistened like a mouth.

THEY STITCHED HIS DAD. That same day, the three of them sat in the backyard and his gramps laid the .308 Winchester across his knees. He cleaned it of water and sand. His dad cradled a mug of coffee in his lap and Winch listened to his gramps's hands clack the mechanical parts, jimmy the bolt to oil it.

—I useta be a pretty good shot, his gramps said, and rubbed a gummy rag along the barrel. —Y'ever fired one of these? he asked, and when Winch shook his head his

gramps came over and looped those old arms around him.
—Keep et tight against yerself.

Winch pressed the wooden stock to the crook of his arm, cupped his hand around the trigger and steadied the muzzle with his palm.

—Ef ya don't keep 'er tight, this'll happen, his gramps said, and touched a crescent scar on the lower cusp of his ocular, about the size of the eyepiece. —S'not a lot of meat between the scope and yer bone, he said.

It felt good, not the weight of it but the power. Winch narrowed his vision to a span the size of a thumb. Things entered that tiny window and then disappeared. When he swung the rifle the world whirred like a slot machine and Winch counted objects as they skipped by: wood chipper, junky Studebaker, oil drums. His finger curled around the trigger. A group of crows rose to the sky, wheeled, pitched toward the Rocky Mountains. His gramps laid a hand on his shoulder. Winch squeezed and held his breath and waited for the rifle to snarl.

A BIG COP WITH dark glasses and a sagging lip swung by with questions because he heard someone got shot. Winch's dad blamed his ex-girlfriend, the mother of his son. The cop nodded and departed, and Winch didn't see Dallas again. According to his dad, Sampson filled the truck with food and supplies and crammed his TV between blankets and a garbage bag of clothes, and with his son beside him he bailed for the East Coast. —Runnin from more 'en just the cops, he heard his dad say.

When Winch entered highschool he began half-hearted attempts at his homework. He passed his classes, if barely. He excelled at tech, woodworking and metal art, and the teacher for both was a dust-haired blonde named Miss Hawk who had enough wrinkles to make her mom-like. She wore scuffed jeans and weathered-down shirts and she had a habit of curling her lower lip over her teeth. Winch wasted hours in her shop while other boys lobbed shot puts, joined basketball teams. Miss Hawk taught him how to bore a stripped screw and the best way to countersink bolts through a steel sheet. Winch earned the right to the school's only chop saw and used it to shave a dowel rod into hexagonal posts for a bird feeder. During metal art he fashioned a wire-frame buggy with workable pistons that pumped when it rolled down a ramp. For machine tech he embarked on a project to rehaul a 1953 Rocket 88 Miss Hawk had rusting in her garage. She told him it belonged to her ex, a welder who took off with a girl half his age. It was the nicest car Winch had ever seen. Miss Hawk and him worked into the bleeding hours nightly. They sandblasted and rewired faults. They polished joints, and Winch recounted his experience of that ancient Chev on the lake bottom at Brisco, how it sort of lingered in his head. Miss Hawk listened with her thumbnail pinched in the corner of her mouth and one knee bent and resting atop a sawhorse. She tossed her hair over her shoulder as he lay on a skid, half tucked under the car. Her overalls swelled at the chest and his eyes could trace her figure despite the baggy clothes. He noticed for the first time the curve of pink skin at her neck so unlike her soot-stained hands. His ears heated and he was thankful to be buried to his ribs under the Rocket 88. For a long time, hers was the body he'd fall back upon in his loneliest nights.

Winch's gramps took to teaching him how to best fire the Winchester. When he came home he'd wing his homework on the kitchen table and head for the backyard. In the distance the Purcells reared ancient and corroded like riverbanks. His gramps set targets on all the junk accumulated on the lawn: oil drums, half a fridge, a trailer nobody ever used. Winch would check and recheck the Winchester, cock the bolting mechanism, and painstakingly blaze those empties to grain. With each shot he'd eject the spent shell and whiff the chamber and its breathy scent of scorched bronze.

At sixteen years old his friends wrangled him to a party at the gravel pits, where he shot straight vodka and finished in a sleeping bag with a pig-tailed girl named Mandy. Her hair smelled like tea leaves and her lips had that cabbage taste of marijuana. Winch had no idea what to do. She wasn't much encouragement. Amid the haze of alcohol and embarrassment and the low, bleating hum of love songs, the only way he could chance an erection was to imagine Miss Hawk with her lips at his cock. Afterward, Mandy jerked onto her side. Figures moved inside trucks and boys stole glances at girls who hadn't covered themselves. Winch listened to canvas and bodies rustle. One last shipping flat was hurled onto the fire. Country ballads rambled from a truck, the bass so thick his heart quivered, and the whole place smelled like alcohol and anticipation.

FOR CHRISTMAS, MISS HAWK presented him with a book called *Layman's Machinist* that contained the schematics for home-built contraptions: a self-making bed; a diesel-fuelled toaster that toasted bread in four and a half seconds; a two-person biplane with an aerofoil constructed from the scraps of a weathervane.

They were late in the shop as usual. Miss Hawk examined a stack of student-built toolboxes at a dinted wood desk, lit with a construction lamp. Winch lay on the concrete, elbow-deep in mechanics. He'd discovered a problem with intake, but with a barbecue lighter and a can of aerosol lubricant he got the engine chortling. Occasionally Miss Hawk snorted at a stupid flaw. She'd cut her hair short – ear length – and dyed it a deep maroon. She wore a yellow dress that hung to her knees. —I don't need to get dirty with you around, she'd remarked when she caught him noticing.

—Winch, she said, and he wheeled himself from beneath the car. —Let's take it for a spin.

Snow covered the ground, inches deep, and more fell from the sky in flakes the size of his big toe.

—The street salt, he said.

—One spin won't corrode it.

He scraped his thumb along a patch of grease on his overalls. They were perpetually damp at the thighs where he wiped his hands and he couldn't drink Coke because the smell reminded him of all that oil.

—Well, Miss Hawk said, and stretched her arms so Winch had to look aside. She dangled two copper-coloured keys from her fingertips. —Come here.

Then he was out of his overalls, in jeans and a sweat-shirt with the school's name – *BTSS* – printed across the chest. He folded into the Rocket's driver seat and Miss Hawk swung in beside him like a girlfriend. Winch strapped himself into the seatbelts that fastened in an X at his sternum. He fit the key in the ignition and leaned on the clutch and the Rocket murmured. Miss Hawk fiddled with the radio for a moment and Steve Miller's "The Joker" hummed from the speaker. He rubbed the stick shift on his palm and then clocked it to reverse, out Miss Hawk's shop and onto Invermere's streets.

He wound around the road by the lake. Snow crunched beneath the tires and air hushed through the trees. Miss Hawk opened her window a finger's width and Winch realized his hands were sweating enough to slicken the wheel. At the beach a huddle of kids passed a spark around. Miss Hawk *tsk*ed and then snaked him a sideways smile. A lone street lamp lit the beach because the frozen lake counted as an actual highway, even if the cops couldn't patrol it.

—Use the lake, Miss Hawk said.

—There's ridges.

—Get you home faster.

Two shallow trenches led over the frozen sand onto the ice. Winch flicked on his highbeams and Miss Hawk reached over and with her thick fingers unclipped his

X-buckle. His cock went instantly hard. —Just in case, she said.

The town lights fell away until his whole world was the space ten feet in front of the car. Miss Hawk's face was lit by reflection off the ice. He pressed his foot onto the gas and the car drew forward, snugged him against the seat. Miss Hawk sucked air through her teeth and braced one hand on the dashboard.

—Faster.

He shifted to fourth in a quick, jerky motion he'd seen men do on television. The car hummed and bucked and the wind from the open windows huffed across his cheek. Miss Hawk flattened her palm against the ceiling and her breasts rose with a held breath and Winch dropped the car to the final gear and laid on the gas and his eyes flickered along the juts and rivets marring the ice's surface.

Lights blinked into view and Winch let off. Sweat pooled in the bowl of his collar. His shirt clung to his back like a tongue. He geared down. Miss Hawk hooked a loose strand of hair behind her ear. They'd drifted from the beaten highway, but the shore in the distance was marked.

—Goes good, Winch said, and Miss Hawk eyed him.

He pulled the Rocket into his gramps's driveway and killed the ignition, and they lingered in the darkness listening to the engine hiss. It was ten o'clock, no later. In the living room blue light danced on a wall, and then a shape rose from the couch and stood at the window – his dad, awake and watching anything so he could see Winch to bed.

—Thanks, Miss Hawk.

She shook her head. —It was all you, Winch.

He climbed from the car as the front door lurched open. His dad stepped out. He wore a pair of jeans and a grey Nike T-shirt. His dad never wore jeans after work, unless he was expecting someone, because he preferred a ratty pair of sweatpants he could lie around in. Miss Hawk's door clunked and she stepped out into the cool air.

—Millie? his dad said.

—Conner? Miss Hawk said.

Winch's dad patted his own head. He scrunched his eyebrows. —What're you doin here?

Miss Hawk circled halfway around the Rocket's grille. She laid one wrist on the hood as if balancing herself.

—Why ya got muh boy with ya? Why're ya – why're ya here?

—Your boy? she said, and then she eyed Winch, lower lip curled over her teeth. She shook her head and puffed air out her lips. —It was a school project.

—Fer what?

—Tech, Winch said.

His dad came down the steps. He tripped and Winch wondered how much he'd had to drink, or worse. —So yer not, his dad said, and reached a hand toward Miss Hawk. —So yer not comin by?

Miss Hawk drummed her heels on the Rocket's bumper. She was sitting on the hood by now. —Fifteen years later, Conner. A change of heart?

His dad's hand swung sideways onto Winch's shoulder.

Those barium-pink fingers dug muscle. —Just when I seen ya here, thought ya were comin by.

—Sorry, Miss Hawk said.

His dad kicked clods of snow free from the driveway.

—Muh boy got what it takes?

—Dad, Winch said.

—Shut it. You're a young buck. More kick 'en yer old man, his dad said, and then spat. —Give 'er a good ride, Winch?

—Conner, Miss Hawk said.

—She tell ya the truth of it? Old Jack, he was gettin nicer tail.

His dad's fingers worked at Winch's shoulder but his eyes were keen on Miss Hawk. She pinned her chin to her chest, clutched a set of keys. She yanked the car door and slipped inside. Winch's dad stepped past him and railed a closed fist on the hood.

—No-good whore, he said, and Winch felt a lump in his throat he couldn't swallow, and he watched his own fist smack his dad in the jaw, an earthy sound, like someone tapping a piece of chalk to slate.

For a moment his dad didn't react. He touched his chin. He glanced from car to woman to boy and then back at the house, his head tilted to the ground and his left eye squinting as though puzzled. Then he shot forward and those two massive pink hands hoisted Winch from the ground.

He landed hip-first, sideways. The impact spiked down his leg. His dad fell upon him, limbs methodical. Winch batted an arm aside, absorbed a half blow with his ribs, snugged his elbow over it. He smelled beer and deodorant and cigarettes, and Winch had never known his dad to smoke.

Then he was rushing upward and the ground left his feet and then he was pinned to a tree. His dad stood below him, nostrils raging. Miss Hawk hollered from the Rocket. His gramps appeared at the front porch, barked: *put him down*. Winch stared at his dad whose fist gyrated in the air and whose forearm pinned him against the tree.

—Nup, his dad said, and lowered him. The fist relaxed, unfurled. He brushed Winch's shoulder, as if to remove dirt. —I won't be that guy.

He faced Miss Hawk. She'd started the Rocket and pulled around to leave. Winch leaned on the tree, a wide trunk, but not the one they built the tree fort on – too old, unsure roots, too much risk. His dad, facing the Rocket, turned his hands out as if to say, *who could've known?*

IN THE MORNING, Winch found his dad hunched at the kitchen table and his gramps pressed into the wedge where counters intersected, arms across his chest. It smelled like charred toast and burned eggs left to soak in the pan. Outside, what little snow they'd had was melted to a great bowel of mud and salt. Condensation pooled on the windowsills and the weak sun beat his dad's shoulders. His gramps plucked the glass eye from its socket and set it on the countertop. It lolled on its side.

—Winch, I didn't mean to scare ya, didn't mean to hurt ya, his dad said. He stared straight ahead and set both his hands on their ridge, fingers stacked upright. —Got some things comin back to me is all.

—Happens, Winch said.

—Might be I need a break, ya know?

His gramps cleared his throat and the phlegm caught like a stalled engine. The glass eye *tink*ed against a ceramic mug. He drew his thumbnail down the scar bisecting his socket.

—Sure, Winch said.

—Didn't know Millie was yer teacher, is all.

—You had a thing?

—Were bad times.

His dad looked anywhere but at him.

—Where ya gonna go? Winch said.

—Won't be away a long time.

—How we gonna get money?

His dad clicked his teeth and his hands rose level with his nose. He pressed them together. —Left yer gramps a stack of cash, sompthen I been savin, just in case.

Winch noticed the hiking pack on an adjacent chair and the puffy balloons of skin hanging over his dad's cheekbones. His hair was greasy and it matted his ears, greyer than Winch could remember, but also thinner, like he'd been tugging at it. His beard had grown and the whiskery hair stained his face like soot.

—I didn't mean to hurchya, Winch.

—Boy knows that Conner, his gramps said.

—I gotta make sure he does.

—He does.

—I'm not leavin fer good, his dad said. He twisted in his chair to face the older man.

His gramps reached for the glass eye, rinsed it under the tap, and popped it in. His eyelid fluttered for a moment and the orb spun. —Winch didn't know that.

—I just told 'im I'm not.

—Awright.

—I just told 'im! his dad said, and slammed his palm on the table.

Winch put his shoulder in the door frame. —Where're ya goin? he said.

His dad slung the pack over his shoulder. It jingled and tinked with items that didn't sound like food and clothes. —Might be I just need a break, his dad said.

After he was gone, Winch stayed in the dark kitchen with his gramps cross-armed at the counter. The old guy watched the floor, chin to chest. Then he plopped the glass eye into his palm and reached for a wallet-sized bottle by the sink and squirted a line of saline solution in the socket. His gramps blinked and wiped a channel of liquid at the corner and said, —Fucken shit always makes my eyes water.

At school Miss Hawk wouldn't look at him. She was in her jeans and roughing shirts, but as he worked wood under a lathe or fit elbows and scored razor edges, Winch pictured her in that yellow dress, the way her face glowed from the ice reflection. —Millie, he mouthed to his metal.

—Millie. He tried staying late, but she told him he had a key now, he could lock, and he spent four hours alone in the garage.

He took up shooting again. Him and his gramps played Donkey, like the basketball game but with rifles. They took turns propping empty Kokanee cans in obscure places on the shooting range: peeking over the lip of the Studebaker's box; half-visible among the branches of a willow tree; suspended on chicken wire so it swayed in the wind like an arm. Winch figured the lone eye gave his gramps an advantage, because the old bastard iron-sighted shots Winch couldn't gamble with a scope. They stocked ammo in a tin cigar case and after their games his gramps rattled the dwindling contents and looked up the road.

Each day he checked the entryway for his dad's steeltoes.

At school, Winch kept with tweak-work on the Rocket, but the spring semester meant new electives he hated but needed to graduate, like art, and biology, and a course called Communication for kids too dumb for real English. The art teacher was a stout woman named Miss Mary Mason who wore a cooking apron and gave the best marks to clever pieces. A deathly skinny kid made a door out of jars and called it *The Door is Ajar*. The preacher's son dismembered plastic dolls and fashioned himself an *Armchair*. Winch couldn't draw and he couldn't paint and he wasted the hour flipping through *Layman's Machinist*, desperate for an idea. He read the article on the home-built biplane. It included a sketch of the product, so he hit Miss Hawk's shop and tried his luck with a miniature. He bolted it together with nail guards, drywall anchors, and an EMT union so it could swivel at the base. Mason graded it a B, said it wasn't art, but good craft. He pawned it to his gramps, who set it on his windowsill beside a banana-sized cactus and a set of dog tags.

His gramps started telling him to make sure the lights were off, his heat dialed down. He started coughing too, at night and in the morning – low, sledge-like sounds while he mulled his coffee.

A girl named Chris with hair the colour of motor oil asked Winch if he'd like to go to a movie. She had compact lips and a dimple more prominent on one side than the other. She said she liked the way he handled things. She said she liked his little biplane. Winch mumbled an acceptance and paid their way to the Toby Theatre on money his gramps thrust into his palm with a wink. The Toby's seatbacks were padded with maroon shag carpet, and overhead, models of World War Two fighters swung from long threads. They pressed hip to hip in a two-person seat and Winch supplied the popcorn and halfway through *Blazing Saddles* they were tongue deep. She tasted like butter and she grabbed incessantly for his hands, and he didn't know why.

IN EARLY SPRING, Chris suggested they sneak to the natural hot springs at the Fairmont resort. One of her brother's friends, a kid they called Squints, tagged along. Squints had curly, pubic-like hair and glasses as thick as a finger. Winch had ideas about the guy, but didn't voice them, swiped his gramps's only bush-lamp, a million-candle beast. When his gramps saw it tucked under his arm, he leaned forward on the couch, where he spent more and more time.

—Ya gonna do sompthen stupid?

—Prolly.

His gramps coughed phlegm and with an apologetic look hawked into a ceramic mug with a picture of two old guys tending a bonfire. He was chalk-white. —I don't wanna waste gas pickin y'up from jail.

—I can hiket.

—Worried about bears?

—Nup.

His gramps lurched upright, hands gripped on his thighs. —Winchester won't stop a bear, anyway, he said, and fingered an empty .308 cartridge centred in a placemat on the table. He tapped his forehead where hair met skull. —Skulls so thick they ricochet bullets an' whatever else.

—Gotta catch 'em in the neck, Winch said.

His gramps shook his head, opened his mouth. —Gums.

Chris drove her dad's Suburban. The journey would take forty minutes, another ten to zigzag to a point where they could hike for the springs. Winch inspected Chris's tires before they hit the road. He remarked that they looked bald as all hell and she flashed him her dad's BCAA card and told him to get in the fucken truck.

They reached a toll booth where a man in a blue blazer wore circular glasses perched too far down his nose.

He peered crow-like at them, slid his window open and dangled one tattooed hand menacingly out the booth.

—Nope, he told them. —Springs are closed for tonight.

—We've got friends at the resort, Chris said.

—Don't think you do.

They retreated. Winch notched his seat forward. Chris hunched over the wheel like a rodent and Squints stayed silent in the backseat and Winch wondered if he planned to contribute anything to the entire trip.

—Could get some booze, Chris said. She pulled onto the shoulder and flicked the cabins on. —I might not get ID'd.

—No, Squints said. In the mirror Winch saw him stretch an arm along the seat. He nodded toward the box and his tongue passed along his teeth and his lip bulged with it. —We can get to the springs guerrilla style. Old guy won't see us. I know some guys doin a party there. Pretend like we're in Vietnam.

—How long? Winch said.

—Hour up, same down.

They left the Suburban in the lot of an A.G. Foods grocery, under a sodium street lamp that lit the silver vehicle like a pumpkin. Squints declared his right to lead. Winch waved him by. As they embarked, Chris told him she'd watched an episode of *Twilight Zone* where a wild-eyed hunter prowled through the forest only to find himself prey to a terrible beast. He tugged her hip against his. When Winch flicked his gramps's massive bush-lamp, Squints ducked as though under fire. —Keep it off, he hissed.

—Awright Sergeant Squints Sir, Winch said, and saluted.

Near the toll the old guy peered through his lenses as if he'd spotted movement. Squints swathed through the brush. Winch held his arm in front of his eyes to catch whipping branches. They appeared on a mountainous road and the resort's lights brimmed in the night sky like fog. Squints passed rubbery water bottles around. Chris circulated a joint. Whenever headlights appeared they barrelled for the ditch, and Winch gashed his elbow in one of the dives.

Chris prodded the skin. —You have thin blood.

—And a thick skull, Winch said.

—Best place to get hit with a beer bottle, Squints said, and rapped his forehead.

Winch's dad had a scar curled over the crest of his forehead, same spot Squints was tapping with his knuckles. After the house burned his mum disappeared, except for one night when she snuck in the rear door of his gramps's place. Winch's dad shovelled stew from his bowl and watched an episode of *Dr. Who*, and though his dad saw her coming, no man alive could have dodged that bottle. Winch looked on from the bedroom where he tucked into the corner with a stray cat named Kalamazoo. Biggest scrap his parents ever dug into, first time he saw real desperation, the way a man gets wild-eyed when he's on the defensive. His dad spent a day laid out with a concussion and two bust knuckles. If he flattened his hand on a hard surface and lifted his middle finger, the bone would rear like a serpent.

They crossed a bridge. Winch grabbed for the fibrous rail and it slickened his palm. A river howled beneath him and the trees on the water's edge shuddered like a drying dog. He hadn't trekked through wilderness for a while. The air hung with dew and the scent of snowfall and the bridge swayed and the moon scythed amid clouds. Halfway across he latched on to the rope rails and braced his legs on the net siding and hoped for a gust to whip the bridge like a sling.

Squints led them down an embankment and Winch went first so he could catch Chris if she took a dive. The air smelled like gunpowder. Chris's shoulder brushed his and he swung his hip into her playfully. Squints soldiered forward with renewed purpose, a bounce to his step like a man planning to get laid. When the springs finally swept into view Squints chortled and pumped his fist in the air. A waterfall splashed to a rocky pool and above it smaller, hotter pools bubbled and steam lilted off them and guys Winch's age and older filled those pools, beer cans clutched talon-like, and empty bottles and cardboard littered around the springs like leaves. He recognized some as jocks, others as the welfare hicks who crowded outside Miss Hawk's shop to catcall her when she walked between classes.

—Squinnnssseeeeyyy, someone bellowed.

In the moonlight a trio of men rose from the hot springs and shambled across the shale that lined the pools. Squints stepped toward them and they clasped hands and Winch realized he did not know Squints's past, what he used to do, which groups he used to hang with. Chris was silent as all hell and she kept one shoulder behind him, her chin to her chest.

—Who's this? the centre man said, and lifted his bottle to indicate Winch. He was the oldest of the three of them, pushing twenty-five, and facial hair horseshoed along his jaw. All three were sleek with the hot water. Steam haloed them. The middle man had a tattoo inked along his neck and down his collar, looping his abs at the ribs, like a belt.

—I'm Winch.

The three men laughed. —Hoi Winch, I'm Lever, one of them said, and they laughed again.

—An' I'm Gearbox.

—An' I'm Stick Shift.

—Good one, Butter, Squints said.

The man in the middle – Butter – rubbed his nose and sniffled loudly. —Who's the cute one in the back? Least ya brought *some* tail.

—She's a friend of mine, Squints said.

—Open season, Butter said.

A gruff voice in the background yelled and Butter twisted halfway, and his exposed cock swung and Winch saw the three men had been skinny-dipping. They all were. —Wanna come fer a swim, baby?

Butter reached across as if for Chris's wrist and Winch knocked his hand away. —Back off, he said.

Butter fingered his beard. Squints sidled away and the two men on either side backed up. Chatter halted in the springs. These were guys who never showed their faces at school but would swarm like maggots at the first whiff of a fight. Winch listened to the waterfall splatter in the largest pool. His dad had told him to pick his fights, because there was no reason to take a shitkicking. A man can tell when things are out of control. In desperation there are no Queensberry Rules.

—Huh, Butter said, as if considering.

Guys climbed from the water and beads trickled down their legs to the pools. The air smelled like a bedroom with no open windows, like ten-ounce boxing gloves with cracked canvas palms. Winch pulled his gramps's bush-lamp to his chest, as if to use it as a shield. Butter fingered his beard again and as he did he eyed Chris. In a few moments Winch would have a dozen other guys atop him.

—Huh, Butter said again.

—Wer leavin, Winch said.

Butter's tongue frogged along his teeth.

—I said wer leavin.

—Yeah? Butter said.

—Didn't know you guys were here is all.

—Think yer takin yer lady friend with ya?

—Thought it was empty up here.

—An' what if I'm gonna give ya a shitkicken fer comin up here? Butter said.

Winch's heart thrummed in his chest and he tightened his grip on the bush-lamp, considered its weight. He linked his fingers around the stiff handle and thumbed the rigid shank, the rubbery slats that provided him grip. It had metal edges, thin barn doors used to funnel light. Butter hunched like a zombie and stroked his fingers along his beard, tongue pinched in the gap between his teeth and his lip.

—I'm just kinda hopin ya don't, Winch said.

—Hopin I don't.

—Yup.

—Hopin I don't take yer lady friend from ya too I bet.

—Yup.

Butter laughed, the other guys with him.

—Yer a funny kid, Stick Shift. A funny kid. Where'd Squints find ya, anyway. Funny kid. Butter nodded toward him. —He's a funny kid eh? The others laughed again and something like a bloodclot balled in Winch's throat, at the divot where his breastbone became his neck, a hard, lumpy knot he had to swallow down.

—Get the hell outta here, Butter said, swiping his hand under his nose. —Get out before I break all yer hopes an' dreams. Y'owe me big, little man, y'owe me big.

He and Chris left Squints with the guys and retraced their steps. Chris fished the remnants of her joint from an inside pocket and offered it, but Winch shook his head and she bagged it. They followed the road. It took longer, and when they passed the toll booth the old guy slammed his palm against the glass. Chris's Suburban still glowed like a pumpkin. They had barely said a word all the way down, the occasional warning at an exposed root or an overhanging branch. Winch slumped in his seat and

Chris waited for two full breaths before she started the ignition.

—Thanks, she squeaked, and he patted her on the thigh, an inch or two higher than they'd established as appropriate.

At home, Chris let him out and rolled down the driveway in neutral, headlamps off. Winch pushed through the front door and kicked his boots into the closet. The living room was dark, but light spilled from the kitchen. He replaced the bush-lamp in the boot closet beside a long-unused fishing pole and a toolbox his dad used to haul down from the shelf before work. His gramps was asleep at the table, forehead to placemat, the .308 disassembled in front of him. Winch capped a tin of polish and a tube of oil and tugged a gummy cloth from his gramps's fingers. He'd never watched the old guy clean the weapon to that extent, never seen the components separated. He recognized the bolt, the tension coil for the trigger, the chamber, and the slick cylinder that locked into the barrel. In his gramps's open palm: a set of dog tags and a .50-calibre shell as long as Winch's thumb – relics whose origins Winch did not know. The firing assembly lay apart, the screws that fastened it scattered, pin disengaged from hinge. Winch fingered the sulphur-scorched hammer and it rattled in its joint, limp, lacking the force he'd known to spark gunpowder.

—Gramps? Winch said, way too loud, and couldn't bring himself to take the old man's pulse.

PAWL

Winch didn't go to school the next day, or the next, or the next. He sat on the couch with the blinds pulled and the Winchester scattered around him. Reassembly of the rifle was beyond him. His hands combed over those scraps of foreign steel. He prodded oiled joints, traced notches, and his palms smudged with the smell of loose change. In tech class Miss Hawk had taught him to troubleshoot mechanics. Work from isolation. Work from causation. Why won't the hammer rise, what's catching the swivel, if he left it to last, would the recoil block still guard against impact? He pulled his gramps's hunting rifle off the wall to deconstruct and analyze, but it was a lever-action, and he couldn't reverse-engineer it. Chris left him messages every hour on the hour. She came by on the second night and he ducked upstairs, to his gramps's room, and she only dared a few steps into the empty house. He wanted to call out to her, to be hugged and comforted by her, but nobody had ever taught him how to ask. It struck him that he was entirely alone.

On the third evening Winch watched headlights flash through a slat in the curtain. Tires churned gravel and a car door whooshed shut and a man cursed. Winch went to the curtains and the light slashed across his face as he peeked through. His dad steadied himself with a hand on the hood of his Sweptline. He reached through the open window and killed the ignition and the lights died.

—Winchy, et's yer dad, he slurred. The front door was locked – to prevent Chris entry – and his dad rattled the rickety thing in its frame. —I dunno where I put muh fucken keys.

—Why ya comin back now? Winch hollered through the wood.

—Muh dad's dead ya dumb cunt. Came back to pay muh dues.

—Ya never called me Winchy before.

—Aww come on.

Winch opened the door and his dad came two steps through and stopped dead as rock. He sucked on breath, and those maimed hands tugged on the hem of his shirt, like a boy. They stayed like that, with the door flown wide. Then his dad eased it shut and pressed his forehead to the wood. —Goddammit, he said.

—I can't rebuild the rifle, Winch said.

—What?

—Gramps's rifle, Winch said. —I can't.

His dad pushed off from the wall. He smelled like a locker room. Winch saw ruddy stains on the sleeves of his dad's T-shirt, frays at the edges, smudges on the collar like oil smears, or unwashed fingers.

Winch went to the kitchen table where he had the rifle parts piled and ordered. His dad followed, the sound of his boots clunking on the lino like a loose timing belt. The two of them sagged into wooden chairs. Winch surveyed the disassembled Winchester, sought similarities among the pieces, hooks and eyes, threads and mouths and notches that could click together like molars. It should've been easy for him. It's what he *did* – it's all he knew how to *do*. His dad pinched a chunk of metal between thumb and index, gave it a twirl. It was jagged, big as a Christmas orange. —Ken ya make some coffee?

Winch put on a pot. His dad massaged his temples, one thumb on each side.

—I done muh best, Winchy.

—Why ya callin me Winchy?

His dad squeezed and unsqueezed that metal part – a component of the stock, if Winch hazarded a guess. —I always call ya Winchy, ya dumb cunt.

—Ya don't never.

—The hell cares about that now, his dad said, and flicked the part aside. —Why ya got this mess here?

—Told ya, Winch said. —I can't rebuild it.

—Can't rebuild what?

—I just told ya. Gramps's rifle. I just said.

—S'just a gun, Winch.

—It's *Gramps's*.

—Awright, his dad said. The coffee blurbled, and Winch lasted a few good seconds of his dad's distant stare before he got up and poured two cups. His dad didn't drink his – only held it in his palm and gritted his teeth.

—Yer a good kid Winch, his dad said. —An' I'm a shitty dad.

—Shut yer mouth, Winch said.

—What're ya goin on about?

Winch sipped the coffee. It burned the roof of his mouth. —Ya don't know me. Ya never even knew me.

—Awright?

—Whatcha want me to say? Winch said.

—I'm a shitty dad, awright?

—Yeah, awright.

—Yeah? his dad said.

—You ain't even said yer sorry.

—Fer what?

—For leavin us, Winch said. He took another sip.
—Chrissakes.

His dad put an elbow on the table. He made a fist, and the knuckles cracked like a ratchet.

—This ent how I thought it'd go.

—How'd ya think, then? Winch said.

His dad just shook his head. —I dunno, Winchy. Like when I got back ya'd be happy to see me or sompthen. That's how et's spose to go. Yer my son, fer fucker's sake. I done muh best.

Winch felt a whole lot bigger all of a sudden. —I dunno, dad, he said.

His dad's face scrunched up, went old, worn out. —I'mma sell this house.

—And where're we goin then? Winch said, but he knew the answer, had known the answer for a long time by now.

—Dunno where yer goin, Winch, his dad said.

—That's why ya came back, then.

—Need to get out.

—Yer my dad.

—Nah Winchy, his dad said, down toward the coffee and the four-fingered hand that gripped it. —Muh dad was yer dad, I didn't do good as him. He got it right or sompthen.

In one of Winch's better memories, he and his dad crouched before a bonfire and tried in vain to make s'mores. They'd just hung the tree fort, and his dad smelled as if he'd been tending a blaze all day. He had a moustache, dark hair that only barely receded past his forehead. Winch was six and his dad seemed noble then, like a man from the nineteen-thirties. They slurped tap water from a steel canteen. They wrestled on the grass, wrapped roasted hotdogs in white bread. And that night they bunked in the tree fort until darkness had settled around them and Winch had drifted asleep with his dad's arm draped over him like a blanket.

His dad pressed a knuckle to his forehead. *Please dad*, Winch wanted to say.

—I'm real sorry, his dad said, and rubbed both eyes with the heels of his palms, and Winch wondered if the good memories would remain, or if they'd all rust down to this dim kitchen, that broken rifle, his weeping dad. The coffee cooled and thickened but when Winch raised it to his lips he still blew across it – an act of denial, because if it was hot, and if it stayed hot, he had reason not to leave the table, and he and his dad could persist as father and son at least a few breaths longer.

WINCH SPENT A GOOD long time with the rifle parts, this time in the dark, while upstairs his dad ruffled through sock drawers and medicine cabinets and the dusty underside of beds in search of who knows what. Winch couldn't fix the rifle – probably never would – but he still liked the weight of the pieces, still liked the way their metal smell chafed onto his calluses and the outside of his hands. So he rolled them around his fingertips, let miscellaneous chunks clack and tick together, let them knock the wood with their hollow baritone sounds. Sometimes he smelled sulphur, or guncotton. Sometimes he heard his dad intake a breath, creak on a floor joist, shut bedroom doors more forcefully than they needed to be shut. The house stayed dark, and Winch stayed still. The fridge hummed, cars trundled by on Invermere's broken streets. Hours later, getting hungry, he rose and moved blindly upstairs to his gramps's bedroom where he found his dad on the bed with a razor and a rail of cocaine laid out on a baking pan.

—So this is it, he said.

—I done muh best, his dad said.

Winch flipped his keys, tried to look anywhere. —I'm goin for a drive.

His dad wiped a sleeve under his nose, sniffled. The room smelled like musk, and semen.

—That's muh truck, Winchy.

—I'm takin a drive.

His dad set the baking pan down, touched his toes to the floor. —I said et's muh truck.

Winch had his wallet and his own set of keys, one of which could operate his dad's truck. He just needed to get there first. —Awright, he said.

—Yer lyin to me, his dad said.

—Am not.

—Winchy, that's *my* truck.

Winch bolted, dragged the door closed behind him and skipped down the stairs in threes. His dad gave chase, clambered out the door and craned heavily into the banister. Winch hit the front door in all-out sprint. —I fucken swear to God, his dad called, but he tripped somewhere in the house and Winch heard the clatter of things knocked askew.

He hauled ass down the driveway. The truck's passenger door was unlocked and he jumped inside and dropped it in reverse. His dad flew out the entryway and lurched a couple steps before he heaved his hands to his thighs and huffed like a man exhausted, and Winch peeled out and felt his dad's eyes trace him all the way around the curve.

He ended up at Miss Hawk's house. His headlights beamed through her front window and movement skipped past the slatted curtains. When she came onto the porch she wore an unflattering dress that hung straight from her shoulders down, men's white socks. Her hair had grown out to its dusty blond, and at a distance, in the low light, she looked like she had the skin of a teenager. Winch dropped from the driver's seat to the ground, her paved driveway. He only knew where she lived because she'd taken her whole tech class, years ago, for a field trip.

—Have you been eating? she said.

—I need to shower or somethin.

—You can come in.

—I'm dirty as all hell.

—Winch, Miss Hawk said, and combed a hand through her hair.

—Muh gramps passed.

—I heard.

—Muh dad just showed up, he's selling the house.

—Why don't you come inside, she said, and pushed the door open a sliver.

Miss Hawk's house was more cluttered than his but it smelled sweeter. A fire burned in her living room. The boot closet brimmed with steeltoes and hikers and a bunched-up pair of Carhartts. Golden Earring's "Radar Love" hummed from a radio in the living room by a butter-coloured couch.

—Bathroom's down the hall, she said. —I was making a grilled cheese. I'll make you one.

He realized he had no toiletries, but it'd been days and he wanted, if nothing else, to *feel* clean in Miss Hawk's house. The bathroom was a tight, storage-sized room with a standing shower and iron decorations. He torqued the hot water crank until steam filled the stall like fog, and fit himself under the tap and let the streams rivet down his chest. The water pounded his skull and he thought about things like money and Chris and if his dad had reported the truck as stolen. Then he heard a thud and the walls shook, and a woman's voice shrilled through the house. He shut the water off. His dad's Sweptline in the driveway, like a trail of goddamned bread crumbs.

—Where is he! Whore, the truck's out front, where is he!

—Get out, Miss Hawk said.

—Millie, his dad growled. —I don't wanna hurchya.

He pictured his dad's lined face, the grey hair and the eyes bloodshot and high. All those years at the barium mine, the hard work, the good example – and now a cokehead like his mother. He wanted to grab his dad's hair and smash that face into a tabletop, until the wood was dented with his dad's front teeth and all that remained in his fist was a bloody husk of hair and sinew.

Winch didn't bother to put on clothes. The adrenalin was in him like an awakening. He stormed out the bathroom and his dad wheeled and said, —There's the pussy.

Winch couldn't have stopped if he wanted to. A great pressure moved him forward. His dad wore a thin grey T-shirt ripped at the collar, blue jeans stained like a drunk's. His eyes were red and wild and open. Winch took long strides, booted a stack of books aside, and with all the upward momentum he could muster he lunged and hooked his dad by the neck, heaved him against drywall. His naked, beaded arm tensed, the muscle strained. His dad latched his fingers, clawed at the grip. It was like the day he watched his dad and mom fight, how his pupils narrowed and his actions went frantic.

Winch backhanded him, hard enough to split his knuckles on his dad's gums.

—Take yer truck an' get out, Winch said through his teeth.

His dad grunted and cold air breezed over Winch's legs, his abs, up his exposed ribs. Miss Hawk stood in the doorway to her kitchen, lit, angel-like, and moved her head once sideways, *no*.

—Get out, Winch said, and let his dad drop to his knees.

—Don't want no boy anyway, his dad coughed, upward.

When he'd gone and Winch had reclaimed his clothes, Miss Hawk dabbed his knuckles with a lukewarm cloth. He'd never had her skin this close to him. Sometimes she moved her hands aside to see him, but he pretended to examine the decor. Her cabinets were deep maroon and she said she painted them herself. A Coke bottle, wrapped in masking tape, centred on the tabletop, plugged with a thin, unused candle. Winch's gramps kept a syrup container covered in glued-on beans as the centrepiece of his table – an art project from his dad's youth.

He didn't realize he was crying until Miss Hawk set the cloth aside and laid her delicate, callused palms on his cheeks.

She locked the door behind them. His cheeks burned as she cinched his shirt in her fist and drew him close. She smelled like she'd been in the shop all day. He clasped her at the waist, unpinned her buttons. She pried his shirt, notched his jeans, and he tightened against the denim. She was square, almost boyish beneath her clothes, stronger than him, and when she clapped her palms on his deltoids his whole body startled at the impact. He trolleyed his lips along her stomach, across her belly button, to the rigid hairs at the fulcrum of her pelvis.

She rocked and shuddered like a truck. When he wedged himself into place a breath trilled through her teeth. Their thighs skidded together. She shifted him, adjusted angles, linked her fingers through his hair. Her nails raked over his ribs. He tended to lower his chin to his chest, stare at her breasts, but she leveraged his head upward with two fingers under his jaw.

Afterward, Winch tucked the sheet under his chin. A horseshoe moon slipped behind clouds. Cars zoomed the Friday streets and their headlamps swivelled through the window like searchlights and Winch pressed his face in the pillow that smelled like Miss Hawk. A tow truck approached from the distance with the distinctive gurgle of diesel and power. Winch waited for it to Doppler. Miss Hawk's pale back faced him and as the tow truck ambled past the window its amber hazards lit her skin like honey. She sniffled, and Winch realized she was weeping. A mole perched on the cusp of one of her vertebrae, another behind her ear. She made a noise, almost like a horse's whinny, and he reached out with tenderness and brushed his knuckles along her spine, but she shimmied forward against her knees and left his hand, cold, in the space between them.

IN A WEEK HE'D have no money, but Miss Hawk would forward his name to a goateed mechanic everyone called Shank, and Winch would receive a phone call, drop from highschool two months before graduation, and start his apprenticeship. While finishing his first year at a community college in Nelson, he'd find out Emily Hawk was knocked up, and he'd count the months backward on his fingers with dread.

But that night he lay awake, naked and spent, and waited, hoping she would circle her tough arms around him. He wanted to feel the taut muscles in her stomach, the swell of her breasts, her nose. As he drifted to sleep he dreamed a future where Miss Hawk birthed a daughter he nicknamed Caboose, where his dad became her gramps, where he built a hangar in his backyard with a concrete floor and a tar-sealed dome in which he undertook a lifelong project to construct a yellow biplane. He would tailor it with two sets of wings and a propeller bolted to the nose, a rudder Miss Hawk would swear he salvaged from weathervane parts. And in that dream he sparked the engine and the plane sputtered and he snugged a pair of aviators over his eyes, and while his daughter and Miss Hawk watched and his dad manned the gunner's seat, those ever-pink fingers strong and patient as a father's, Winch took off in a contraption he'd hand-built to carry him from the earth.

ACCELERANT

A long time ago I shot Mike Twigg in the back with a potato cannon. We were getting shitfaced on flats of Kokanee at the marsh behind my buddy's house. Twiggy dove sideways even as I grabbed for the cannon, but only his head and shoulders had cover behind the upturned lawn table when my thumb found the igniter. The potato *thoowunk*ed from the barrel and a husk of pool noodle floundered behind it – we used it as stock – and I watched the projectile beeline for the bastard's kidney. It cracked him pretty good and he spewed curses like a foreman, but I just disengaged the chamber and sniffed the residue accelerant. —You deserve every goddamned shot, I yelled.

Twiggy had violated the Code. Nowadays he pawns it off as a mere cock-block but it was more than that. Twigg, with his screwdriver-blade eyes and that smile like a bullmastiff, kiboshed my first real chance at losing the V-card, and to Ash Cooper of all people; I can still see those red bangs and the ponytail as it bobbed up and down the soccer field. Twiggy tells me to shut my yap because it's not his fault I couldn't wrangle another girl before college, but let me just say that the school of freshwater fish is pretty limited in Invermere, B.C.

Twiggy trench-crawled on the dirt as I breeched another round into the cannon. I hear stories about guys who fashion "spud guns" that shoot thumb-sized morsels with compressed air. We dubbed ours a *cannon* because we'd constructed an ABS beast that launched whole potatoes with the power of propane combustion. I locked the chamber into place, injected a few hisses, and hefted the cannon onto my shoulder.

—Matt, Twigg says up at me. —Matt, come on.

Then I hear my pal Duncan laugh from the roof of his house, a dumpy panelboard bungalow that used to be a laundromat. He's got a view of us from up there. Twiggy yells for help and Duncan says, —Yeah, I'll help you, but he doesn't move. I level the cannon where I suspect Twigg's ass is, though I can't be sure because I'm shitfaced and because Twigg has come into possession of a campaign sign for the local election – there's a pile of them ditched into the marsh, another story – and spread it over his crotch for defence. I pinch one eye shut and sight down the barrel at the salesman grin of Don Chabót, Conservative Party.

Me and Ash dated for a couple weeks before Twigg ruined it. I'd ferreted her from this goody-goody named Will who thought himself tough because his old man was a cop. I pegged him as a pushover. Ash had freckles and a small upturned nose and muscled arms, the kind of grey, appropriately spaced eyes that always seemed a tad disappointed in everything I had to say. Progress with her was slow but gradual, the occasional palm on her flat stomach but no further, maybe a glance down her shirt while we made out. Most evenings we'd do things like skirt the lake and examine odd-looking driftwood or loiter at the gelati café to sip coffees with long-winded names.

That particular and devastating day she'd come to hang out with me and Twigg and Duncan to drink beers and shoot shit. Now I've known Twiggy for the better part of a long time and his luck with girls is ill-fated at best. You might say there's a disconnect between him and the knowledge of what girls like. We're up on the roof with a flat of Kokanee and the potato cannon. Duncan blares one at the vast nothingness of the marsh and it shrinks to a dot against the Rocky Mountains. We pass the cannon around. Even Ash takes a go. On my turn I crack the chamber and tear a hunk of pool noodle and cram it in behind the potato. I lift the beast beside my ear. Across the street there's a gas station and the dumbasses who work the till have misspelled "3 cents of at pump." I take aim at the missing *f* and smell the tarry ABS and feel the horizon on my cheek and it is then that Twigg drops my pants. I don't mean only my pants – the whole mechanism. Jeans, belt, boxers. I'm awhirl in the breeze and Twigg's got this shit-eating grin and Ash makes a noise like a cat about to hawk.

I chased her down the street like a married man. When she stopped we were on a bridge over a railroad and beneath us a train trundled along the track. I think: alright, damage control, like my dad used to preach. But Ash won't hear it. —Sorry Matt, she says, this look like she's about to turn down a loan. —You're just too much of a *boy*.

So Ash is ten-thirty-five and I've got Twigg on the ground and the cannon on my shoulder. Don Chabót's double chin fills my crosshairs and I wonder how Twigg figured the campaign sign would help his cause. The potato blows that dopey smile to hell and Twigg shrieks, and he shrieks again, this savage, desperate sound I've only heard mimicked one time since: a woman who screamed *He's choking!* to a full restaurant in Miami. Duncan scrambled down from the roof. Twigg had gone fetal on us.

Testicular torsion is not a pretty thing to even say. It is a twisting of the spermatic cord identified by moderate to high discomfort and the restriction of blood flow to the nut-sac, a medical emergency. Neither Duncan nor I were in any shape to drive. We made a few phone calls. Twigg got to the hospital in time. The doctors opened him up and did what they had to do and later he'd tell us he felt the knife go in.

Not much remains of those summers. Duncan's gone, dumb bastard, and our old binge grounds have been wrecking-balled. That limitless marsh has parched up and nowadays the hardware stores won't sell boys a length of ABS pipe. Maybe the town has moved on. I only see Twigg every couple years, and last I heard he'd set up shop on the East Coast where he explosion-proofs submarines. I guess that's the way things go. Though we'll talk about her over beers, neither of us are really sure what happened to Ash Cooper. Maybe she ended up with her cop-son husband, still in old Invermere, twisted into the nostalgia of it all.

—Small-town girls, Twigg might mumble into his pint. —They come into your life and then they're gone and you've forgotten them just as quick. You know how it is, Matt. You know how it is.

THE DEAD ROADS

One time we roadtripped across the country with Animal Brooks, and he almost got run over by a pickup truck partway through Alberta. It was me and my twenty-year-old girlfriend Vic and him, him in his cadpat jumpsuit, Vic in her flannel logger coat and her neon hair that glowed like a bush-lamp. We'd known Animal since grade school: the north-born shitkicker, like Mick Dundee. A lone ranger, or something. Then in 2002 the three of us crammed into his '67 Camaro to tear-ass down the Trans-Canada at eighty miles an hour. Vic and me had a couple hundred bucks and time to kill before she went back to university. That'd make it August, or just so. Animal had a way of not caring too much and a way of hitting on Vic. He was twenty-six and hunted looking, with engine-grease stubble and red eyes sunk past his cheekbones. In his commie hat and Converses he had that hurting lurch, like a scrapper's swag, dragging foot after foot with his knees loose and his shoulders slumped. He'd drink a garden hose under the table if it looked at him wrong. He

174

once boned a girl in some poison ivy bushes, but was a gentleman about it. An ugly dent caved his forehead and rumours around Invermere said he'd been booted by a cow and then survived.

Vic stole shotgun right from the get-go and Animal preferred a girl beside him anyway, so I'd squished in the back among our gear. We had a ton of liquor but only a two-man tent because Animal didn't care one way. He'd packed nothing but his wallet and a bottle-rimmed copy of *The Once and Future King*, and he threatened to beat me to death with the Camaro's dipstick if he caught me touching his book. His brother used to read it to him before bed, and that made it an item of certain value, a real point of civic pride.

The Camaro's vinyl seats smelled like citrus cleaner. First time I ever got a girl pregnant was in Animal's backseat, but I didn't want to mention it since Vic would've ditched out then and there. Vic'll crack you with a highball glass if you say the wrong thing, she can do that. We weren't really dating, either. She just came home in the summers to visit her old man and score a few bucks slopping mortar, and we'd hook up. I don't know anyone prettier than Vic. She's got a heart-shaped face and sun freckles on her chin and a lazy eye when she drinks and these wineglass-sized breasts I get to look at sometimes. On the West Coast she bops around with a university kid who wears a sweater and carries a man purse. Her dad showed me a picture of the guy, all milk-jug ears and a pinched nose that'd bust easy in a fight. Upper-middle-class, horizon-in-his-irons, that type. Not that I can really complain, I guess. Vic never mentioned him and I never mentioned him and we went about our business like we used to, like when we were sixteen and bent together in the old fur-trading fort up the beach on Caribou Road.

Vic planned our journey with a 1980s road atlas she snagged from her dad's material shed. Animal kept his hand on the stick shift so he could zag around semis hauling B.C. timber to the tar sands. Whenever he geared to fifth his palm plopped onto Vic's thigh. Each time, she'd swat him and give him the eyebrow and he'd wink at me in the rearview. —Dun worry, Duncan, I wouldn't do that to ya, he'd say, but I know Animal.

For the first day we plowed east through the national park. Cops don't patrol there so Animal went batshit. His Camaro handled like a motorbike and it packed enough horse to climb a hill in fifth, and I don't know if he let off the gun the whole way. He held a Kokanee between his legs and gulped it whenever the road straightened. Animal was a top-notch driver. As a job, he manned a cargo truck for this organic potato delivery service. One time he spun an e-brake slide at forty miles per hour, so me and him could chase down these highschoolers who'd hucked a butternut squash through his windshield.

To kill time, Animal bought a *Playboy* and handed it to Vic. He suggested she do a dramatic read if possible. At first she gave him the eye, but he threatened to have me do it if not her. He also handed her all the receipts for gas and food and booze to keep track of, on account of her higher education, but I'm not even sure Vic did much math. At university she studied biology and swamplands, and I like to think I got her into it, since there's a great wide marsh behind this place we used to get shitfaced at. It's a panelboard bungalow on the outskirts of town, built, Vic figures, on floodland from the Sevenhead River. Vic and me used to stash our weed in the water, pinned under the vegetation band. One time we stole election signs and ditched them in the marsh, and the *Valley Echo* printed a headline that said the cops didn't know to call it vandalism or a political statement. Neither did I really, since Vic planned the whole thing. Then last summer I asked her to muck around the marsh with me but she said we really shouldn't, because it's drying up. She had a bunch of science to prove it. —Something has to change, Dunc, she said, pawing at me. —Or there'll be nothing left.

Eventually Animal bored of the Trans-Canada, so he veered onto some single-lane switchback that traced the Rocky Mountains north. I thought Vic'd be distressed but turned out she expected it. She shoved the road atlas under the seat and dug a baggie of weed from her pack. Later, we played punch buggy, but I couldn't see much from the back and Vic walloped me on the charley horse so goddamn hard I got gooseskins straight down to my toes.

THE SIGN SAID, *Tent Camping – $15*, and Animal said, —Fuck that shit, and then he booted the sign pole, for good measure. He plunked himself on the Camaro's cobalt hood and rubbed his eyes. We'd been on the road for a while, and I don't remember if he ever slept much. The air smelled like forest fire and it also reeked of cow shit, but Alberta usually reeks of cow shit. Vic leaned into the door frame, hip cocked to one side like a teenager. Her flannel sleeves hung too low and she bunched the extra fabric in each fist. She chewed a piece of her hair. When we used to date I would tug those strands out of her mouth and she'd ruck her eyebrows to a scowl and I'd scramble away before she belted me one. It was starting to turn to evening. In the low Albertan dusk her bright hair shone the colour of whiskey. She caught me staring, winked.

Vic slid her hands in her jean pockets. —I got fifteen bucks.

—Yeah I bet ya do, Animal said.

—What the hell does that mean?

—Et's Duncan's cash, enn'it?

—Just some, Vic said.

—I got more money 'en Duncan, ya know.

—Shut your mouth, Animal, I told him.

—Jus sayin, he said, and ducked into the driver seat.

We reached someplace called Shellyoak and Animal called all eyes on the lookout for a campsite. He drove through the town's main haul, where the Camaro's wide nose spanned the lane past centre. A ways out, the Rockies marked the border home. This far north their surfaces were dotted with pine husks – grey, chewed-out shells left over from the pine beetle plague. Not a living tree in sight. Shellyoak's buildings were slate brick with round chimneys and tiny windows high as a man's chin. A group of kids smoked dope on a street bench and Vic hollered for directions and one waved up the lane with an arm so skinny it flailed like an elastic. —Near the amusement park, he called.

Big rocks broke the landscape on Shellyoak's outskirts, and Vic figured it used to be under a glacier. Animal was dead silent the whole way. I guess the bony trees irked him, that carcass forest. The stink of woodsmoke blasted from the fan and it reminded me of the chimneys that burned when I used to scrape frost off Vic's windshield, all those mornings after I stayed the night at her place. One time her dad was in the kitchen as I tried to sneak out, and he handed me a coffee and some ice shears and told me to keep in his good books. Then he said Vic and me made a good pair, us two, but if I got her pregnant he'd probably beat me to death with an extension cord. He grinned like a boy, I remember. Then he said, —Seriously though, ya make a good pair. A few minutes later Vic tiptoed downstairs and her old man clapped me on the shoulder like a son, and Vic smiled as if she could be happier than ever.

Animal yawed us around a bend and all at once the horizon lit up with a neon clown head big as an RV. From our angle, it looked as if the clown also had rabbit ears, flopped down like two bendy fluorescent scoops. The highway'd gone gravel and the Camaro's tires pinged pebbles on the undercarriage. In the distance I saw a Ferris wheel rocking like a treetop, but not much else in the park to speak of. Animal geared down and this time when he laid his palm on Vic's knee he didn't take it off, and she didn't smack him. He still winked at me in the rearview, though. A second later Vic shook his hand away.

—Christ, it's a gas station too, Vic said, pointing at the pumps hidden in the clown's shadow. Animal steered toward them, tapped the fuel gauge with its needle at quarter-tank.

—You've got enough, I said, but he didn't so much as grunt.

He parked at the first pump and unfolded from the vehicle. Vic popped her seat forward so I could climb out. Figures milled inside the gas station and their outlines peered through the glass. A painted sign that said *Tickets, 5 bucks* hung above the door. On it, somebody'd drawn a moose. Animal started pumping gas. He tweaked his eyebrows at me. —Well?

—The hell do you want now, I said.

—Go enside and ask where we ken camp, he said. He winked over my shoulder, at Vic. —Giddyup now.

—They'll tell us to go to the pay grounds.

—Kid said we ken camp near the amusement park.

—That kid was on dope, I said.

—Yer on dope, he shot, and *thrump*ed his fingers on the Camaro's hood. He flashed his gums. —Go on, Skinny.

—What the fuck, Animal.

—Yer in muh way, Skinny, he said, and cocked his head to indicate Vic. —I seen better windows 'en you.

Then the station's stormdoor clattered and Vic yelped and I turned and saw the biggest goddamn Native man ever. He wore Carhartts and steeltoes and no shirt beneath the straps. The buckles dimpled his collar. His hair gummied to his cheeks and his head tilted at an angle. This gruesome, spider-like scar spanned his chest and the whole left nipple was sliced off, snubbed like a button nose. He leaned an arm-length calliper on his neck. Then his face jerked into a smile, but not a friendly kind. —I never seen a Camaro can run on diesel, he said, stressing his *e*'s.

For a second he stood there in the doorway as if he might say *gotcha!* Vic bunched excess sleeve in her fists and I sniffed the air to see if the place reeked like diesel engines. And there it was: the smell of carbide and tar and dirty steel. Animal stared straight at the Native guy, as if in a game of chicken instead of wrecking his engine with the wrong fuel, as if he just needed to overcome something besides the way things actually were, as if he could just *be* stubborn enough. Then he killed the pump and yanked the nozzle from his tank. —Where the fuck's et say?

The guy did a shrug-a-lug. —It's a trucker stop.

—Yeah well I'm notta trucker.

—Me neither, the guy said, and moved between Vic and me, toward the car, and the air that wafted after him stunk of B.O. His neck muscles strained to hold his head straight, like he was used to keeping it down. A scrapper's stance, almost. I caught Vic's attention and her forehead scrunched up and the skin at her eyes tightened like old leather. I'd never known her to be the worrying type.

—Nice car though, the guy said. He dragged a wide hand over the Camaro's cobalt finish.

—Yeah et is.

—I'm Walla, he said, and swung his head to Vic. —This your girlfriend?

Animal banged his commie hat against his knuckles. —Ya got a pump er sompthen?

—Nup, Walla said, and stressed the *p*.

—Or sompthen else?

—Buddy has a siphon.

—Ken we get et?

—Nup, getting too late, he said, and pointed with one sausage finger at the darkening sky. —Tomorrow, I bet.

Animal's mouth jawed in circles and I could all but hear his brain trying to find a way to make it all go right. —There a campsite nearby? I said, to buy time.

Walla twitched his head behind him. —The summit. Not like she's a real mountain, though. You owe me twelve thirty-seven for the diesel.

—The hells I do, Animal said, and crossed his arms.

Walla set the callipers on the Camaro's hood and their measurement end *tink*ed. He swung his gaze from me to Animal to Vic, then to Animal and then at the shop. He stood nearest Vic of all, a full two and a half heads taller than her, and I swear to God he had hands big as mudflaps. —No, he said, very slowly, —you do.

Vic dug cash from her wallet, fifteen bucks. She handed it over and Walla tugged the bills one at a time. —I'll get your change, he said, and stepped toward the station. Then, over his shoulder: —You can't leave your car there. He grinned at Vic and his teeth were white as gold. —Well, maybe you can. Push her outta the way of the pump.

I got behind the Camaro. Animal hung at the gas tank like one of those old guys who hope somebody'll come talk to them. —Put her in neutral, idiot, I snapped, and dug my toes into the ground and heaved and the Camaro rocked. Vic pressed her back to the bumper. —What's happening? she whispered to me, but I grunted and got the car rolling and hoped I didn't have to scrap with Walla.

We pushed the Camaro outside the clown face's shadow and I put myself between Vic and the station. Walla reappeared, horselike in his gait. He dumped the coins in my palm and ran his tongue over his teeth. He touched a notch under his jaw. —The summit'd be a helluva climb, he said. —Especially if you're taking your booze. I got a pickup.

—We can hike it, I said.

—Trade you a lift.

—Fer what, Animal barked.

—What ya got? Walla said, and rubbed his triceps. The scar tissue on his chest looked sun-dried, pinker than it ought to, and in the sticky neon light it shone raw and oily like a beating. —Aw hell, he said, —I'll help you out. Get yer stuff.

We grabbed our beer cooler and Vic took the sleeping bag and Animal pocketed *The Once and Future King*. Walla disappeared around the gas station and a few minutes later he came chewing up gravel in a green three-seater Dodge. He was sardined in driver with his shoulders hunched and his knees against his armpits. The truck had a bust-out rear window and poly duct-taped in the gap. Horse quilts blanketed the box, warm with the smell of dog.

—One of you needs to sit in the bed, Walla said, then dangled his keys, —and one of you needs to drive, cause I'm shittered and the fucking pigs have it out for me.

Animal lunged for the keys and me and him shared this moment between us, his mouth twisted like a grin, and I wanted to hit him so bad. But if I whaled on him I'd look bad to Vic, so I climbed into the mess of bedding while Animal drove the switchback. The truck whipped around bends and I imagined Walla's skunky B.O. sneaking through the patched-up window, how bad it must've been in the cab with him. Animal was goddamn lucky he'd pocketed his book. The whole way, Vic shifted uncomfortably, and I could hear her thighs brushing Walla on one side and Animal on the other.

WE GOT TO THE summit when the sun tucked under the Rockies and everything went grey and dead-looking as the forest. Walla showed us a firepit ringed by skeleton trees where he'd piled some chopped wood. Animal collapsed near the pit to work a blaze. He waved Vic off when she offered to help, so she dug a mickey of Canadian Club from the cooler. Fifty feet off, a cliff dropped to the highway below, where the Ferris wheel keeled and the goddamn clown face smirked.

—Thanks for helping us, Vic said. She sat down on an upturned log, whiskey on her knee.

—My dad tells me if you're cooking stew, and you don't put meat in it, you can't bitch when yer eating it, Walla said, and he grinned to show his pearly teeth, and Vic laughed and so did I, though I didn't know what the hell he meant. Then he said: —Now I need a lift down to the station.

Vic froze in the middle of sipping her whiskey and Animal looked up from his smouldering fire. —What'dya mean.

—I told you, I'm shittered, and the pigs have it out for me.

—I'm buildin the fire, Animal said, but Walla had his eyes on Vic, anyway. Vic glanced from Walla to me and I knew she wouldn't ask me to step in, because she won't do that, ever. One time she figured out how to fix a circuit fault on her Ranger all on her own, because she didn't want to ask her old man how.

—I'll do it, I said to Walla, and then I dumped my half-empty beer over Animal's wimpy fire and he threatened to beat me to death with the kindling.

Walla flicked me his keys and I palmed them from the air and got in the driver seat, and he swung into passenger like a buddy. Not thirty seconds into the drive his stench soured up the cab, but at least he smelled like a working man, like he just forgot to shower, and not like some hobo. On the way down, the poly over the rear panel smacked about and more than once he leaned sideways to inspect the tape. He spread one leg across the seat, draped his arm clear out the window, and I wondered if his knuckles bobbed along the gravel. In the distance, the horizon glowed from the park lights and the treetops resembled hundreds of heated needles. I kept the highbeams on and scanned for marble eyes, since twilight is the worst time for hitting deer, but Walla told me that all the deer fled north with the beetles. —Nothin here but us and the flies, he said. —A thousand dead acres.

—The dead roads, or something.

—I don't mind that, Walla said. Then: —They're an odd couple, eh?

—Who.

—The girl and him, Animal.

—They're not a couple.

—The way he looks at her? Sure they are. Or gonna be, he said, and punched me on the arm like we were friends.

—He looks at all girls like that.

Walla smiled like a Mason jar. He had fillings in his teeth. —Her, too. She was lookin at him too.

The station and the clown face swept into view, and as I geared down my fist touched Walla's knee. Vic had about zero reason to go for a guy like Animal, so I don't know. But then I imagined the two of them bent together at that shitty fire, red marks scraped over Vic's neck and collar-bones from Animal's barbed-wire stubble.

—You got a thing for her, eh, Walla said.

—No.

—Might be you need to take him down a notch.

—We're buds, I said, and parked the truck.

Walla extracted himself from the passenger seat. —Nah man, he said across the hood. —*We're* buds.

Whatever the hell he meant I'll never know, since I ditched him and started back along the road, toward the summit. The whole way I thought about Animal and Vic and I tried not think about them at the same time. I'd known them so long – my two best friends, really. The outside smelled more like driftwood than a forest. Wind kicked dirt at my face and though it breezed around the treetops they just creaked like power poles. I wouldn't have been surprised if a goddamn wolfman came pounding out of the dark. A few times headlights tear-assed up the road and a few times I almost barrelled sideways and I just got madder even thinking of it.

Then the slope evened out, which meant I neared the summit, and then the trees flickered campfire-orange. The road looped our campsite so I cut through the forest. Never been so scared in my life, those last steps. Animal atop Vic, grinding away, probably still in his stupid commie hat and his Converses – no sight in the world could be worse. I'd rather get shot. Walla was right – Animal'd been gunning for her the whole trip. Right from the start when he kicked me to the backseat, some big plan – some big, selfish plan.

I got close enough to see the flames. Vic sat under her sleeping bag, off near the cliff edge, but I could only make out her outline in the orange light. Animal was MIA. They might have already finished, how could I know. I crept along the tree line, scanned for him. Not sure what I hoped to accomplish. It's not like he kept a dark secret.

I found him outside the campsite with his back to the slope and his cock in his hand and a stream of piss splattering on a tree. It was dark enough that I didn't get the whole picture, thank God for that. He'd crossed the road to make use of a big pine that might have been a little bit alive – for some reason Animal really didn't like those dead trees. I had some things to say to him. Vic's old man once told me a guy needs to know when to pick his battles, and as I watched Animal, pissing as if nothing mattered, I figured it out: a guy needs to know what he cares about most, and Animal, well, he didn't care about stuff. But he had to know I did. Christ, everybody in the valley knew I did. It'd be like if I tried to steal his car for a joyride. I'm his friend, for fucker's sake.

Then a truck hauled ass up the road, kicking gravel in a spray. It had a good clip and its rear end fishtailed, out of control or so the passengers could get a laugh. Its headlamps swung around, but on that switchback the dead trees scattered the light – no way the driver would see Animal, not before clobbering him. Animal turned as if to check what the commotion was about. Either he couldn't see or he was too stupid to dive for cover or he figured no truck would dare to run him down. I saw the trajectory, though, loud and clear: the pickup's rear end would swing into him, knock him ass-over-teakettle into the woods, and that'd be that for Animal Brooks. But I didn't yell out. I didn't make a sound. Because all I could think of was his hand on Vic's thigh, over and over the whole trip, his wild grin in the rearview and all the stuff he'd pulled to be alone with her. So nope, I didn't yell out, and the truck fishtailed right toward him and he yowled like a dog and I lost track of where he went.

Vic bolted from the tree line, almost right into me, and I scrambled after her. She gave me a look, as if surprised, but I just nodded like I ought to be there. Animal had already clambered to his feet. Moss and dead twigs stuck to his face, and his commie hat had been biffed away and the forest floor was beat up where he'd rolled across it. He pulled a pinecone from his hair and stared at it in wonder.

—Animal, Vic barked. —You okay?

He flicked the pinecone aside, seemed to notice us. —Why the hell didn't ya say sompthen, he said, staring at me.

—What?

—Yuh were across the road. Why didn't ya yell out or sompthen. Fucken truck nearly killed me.

—I just got here, I told him.

—Ya just got here, eh.

—Yeah, got back right now.

Animal swiped his commie hat from the ground. He banged it against his thigh to dust it off. —Just en time to see my kung fu reflexes, he said, and grinned.

—So you're okay? Vic said.

—Shaken up, yeah.

Vic grabbed Animal's chin and turned his head sideways. His cheek was scraped and dirty and Vic licked her thumb to rub it clean. —Mighta pulled a groin muscle, too, he said when she stepped back, and Vic lasted a full two seconds of his leer before she punched him in the chest hard enough to make him wheeze.

AFTERWARD, BY THE FIRE, Animal shook out his adrenalin. —Woulda sucked to run that truck over, he said, and laughed, a deep, throaty laugh like a guy does when he's survived an event that should have killed him. Then he dug into the cooler and started skulling beers to drown his jitters.

Vic and me shared the mickey of Canadian Club, away from the campfire so we could look over the cliffside at this bizarre piece of land. She took a big chug from the bottle and handed it over. Vic can drink like a tradesman when times come. The moonlight made her cheeks silver and that lazy eye of hers acted out. She spread her sleeping bag across her legs and I inched my way under it and the nylon clung to my shins. Vic smelled like a campfire. Vic smelled like citrus shampoo or something. Vic smelled like Vic.

—This an alright place to sleep, she said and wiggled in the dirt and the dried bloodweed and made a little nest.

—I'm not picky, I said.

—You smell like a dog.

—Sorry, Vic.

She belted me on the shoulder and I leaned into her. Below us a couple semis zoomed north and the Ferris wheel spun and I thought I could hear Walla chopping lumber. Christ, a weirder place. By the fire, Animal sounded out words from his book, finger under each sentence. Then Vic unbuttoned her flannel coat. She always wore it or if not the coat then a flannel shirt. Sexiest thing, swear to God. I remember how she took it off, first time we ever boned,

190

all awkward and struggling so I had to help her with the sleeves. A different kind of time back then. A different way of going about things, even. Sometimes I wish I was smarter so I could've gone to university with Vic.

Vic put her hand under my chin and jacked my head to eye level. I guess I was looking at her breasts. She leaned in and kissed me and she tasted like dope, and softness, and her smooth chin ground on my middle-of-the-night stubble. But I couldn't kiss her right then. I don't know why. She slicked her tongue over my lips and I couldn't get my head around the whole thing, the Ferris wheel and what Walla said and how I almost got Animal killed, and Vic, you know, and the whole goddamn thing.

—Don't fuck around, she said, but the words were all breath.

—Just thinkin is all.

She bit down on my lip. —Well, stop it.

—I like you a lot, Vic.

For a second she stopped and turned her head and her neon hair grazed my nose and I'd have given anything to know what was going on in her head right then. She had her lips squished shut and her forehead a little scrunched as if figuring something out - same look as the day she left for university. That'd have been in '99, and her and her old man and me stayed at a hotel in Calgary so she could catch her West Coast flight in the wee hours, and while she showered, her old man told me not to let her get away. —It'll happen, Duncan, he said, his face drawn in and lined around his eyes, as if he knew what the hell he was talking about. —I swear to God you'll lose her if you don't take action soon. And I nodded and tried not to grin, because I understood exactly what he meant.

On the mountaintop, Vic hooked hair behind her ear. —You're my guy, Dunc, she said as though it were true.

—I know, Vic. But sometimes I don't know. You know?

Then she cuffed me, all playful, and pulled me into her.

But that's Vic for you. Afterward, when we were done and Animal's moans were snores and the fire glowed down to embers, Vic sat up and stretched. Her ribs made bumps under her skin and the muscles along her spine tensed and eased and it felt alright right then. That's Vic for you, that's how she can make you feel, that easy. Never liked a girl so much. Nothing else to it. I just cared about her more than the university guy did or Animal did or maybe her old man did. I should've told her so, or how I wished she didn't have to go west, or how I'd had a ring for her for years but lacked the balls to do anything with it. Even then, the mountaintop seemed like a last chance or something.

She sucked the rest of the whiskey and pointed at the sky where a trail of turquoise streaked across the horizon – the northern lights, earlier than I'd ever known them. She just stood there for a second with her back to me and those lights around her. Christ, she was so pretty. Then she whipped the empty bottle off the summit, and I stared at her and thought about her and waited for the sound of the bottle breaking way, way below us.

THE MILLWORKER

Mitch parked his old Ranger in front of the garage door and shifted the clutch to first, killed the ignition. His e-brake had gone slack and this worried him: a couple months ago his son's Taurus rolled down the driveway and butted up to a tree across the road. It could have been a mess but Mitch was awake in the bleeding hours – first guy out of bed on the whole street, on his way to the mill – to wake Luke before anything went south.

Nobody had left any lights on for him but he'd grown used to this kind of inconsideration. He eased himself from the Ranger, imagined his muscles unfolding like big ropes. Everything was the colour of ink. The sun teased behind the Rockies, gave tungsten outlines to their silhouettes. Invermere's streets were quiet save a herd of deer plucking crabapples from a neighbour's tree. Mitch knew guys who'd rather blare a hollowpoint into a deer than let it eat their fruit, and why those guys lived in the Kootenay Valley he couldn't say. They might as well head east, leave B.C. There was plenty of room in the tar sands.

Inside, Mitch tugged off his heavy, grease-grimed boots, and they left his fingers gummy when he knelt to unknot the laces. About the only thing he wanted was a beer and a nap, but not a dozen steps out of the entryway the kitchen fixture wouldn't turn on, and it was probably something Andie already told him about, something he should've fixed days or weeks ago, so he grabbed a chair and wiggled the curly fluorescent bulb and it flared to bright, and he blinked turquoise spots from his eyes. The kitchen smelled like cinnamon and his wife. Overhead, wallpaper banded the ceiling, patterned with chickens and leopards and zebras and giraffes. The guys at the mill would give him hell for that, but it kept Andie happy.

Mitch bent backward at the hip until his spine popped and the tension lessened. It'd been an extra eight hours shoving lumber and he was gamy with the smell of sawdust and that metallic thing tools do to your hands. Everything ached. Invermere's was about the only mill in all B.C. that hadn't gone fully auto – valley stubbornness, valley fascination with relics. He shrugged his coat over the back of a kitchen chair. It used to be his dad's, that coat, and over the years Mitch had sewn its holes and fixed its tears and patched it with reflectors so the late-shifters wouldn't knock him blindly into a presser. Whenever he caught flak from the young bucks who strutted around invincible, Mitch reminded them of the kid whose legs got crushed so bad that bone fragments ravaged his blood-stream like grains of mortared glass.

He dug his gloves from the coat's gut pocket and tossed them in the laundry sink. Splinters jutted from the palms, not deep enough to gouge his skin. He'd thank God for that, if it mattered – little in the world disgusted him more than slivers. Once, during a dry summer in his childhood when he romped through the wilderness like a kid ought to, a buddy of his snagged a wood shard in his palm, fat as a pencil, and the hand swelled up like a boxing glove. It had something to do with wood pulp, something to do with allergies, but that ballooning hand stayed radiant in Mitch's memory.

He collapsed on the couch in his dirty overalls knowing Andie would give him hell, and, as if sensing him through the ether, upstairs a light flicked on. Andie descended, hand trailing on the banister. She wore a forest-green bathrobe that, when pulled closed, would display a logo of a windmill with a great, proud *S* in its centre. Mitch bought it for her three years ago to celebrate the rebranding of the Calgary Flames into the Saskatchewan Windfarmers – her homeland's first NHL team since its failed bid for the Saskatoon Blues almost five decades earlier, in the eighties.

Andie's brown hair hung to her shoulders and Mitch stared at her like always. He'd never known anyone who could be so beautiful first thing in the morning. Her nose bent a little sideways – she broke it, years and years ago, with her own knee – but she had the creamy skin of a movie star. She put her shoulder against the wall. Her bathrobe swayed open but she cinched it shut. The small lines around her eyes and at the corners of her lips made her look older than she was. He probably had something to do with that.

—It's cold, she said.

Mitch leaned forward on his thighs. —I can turn up the heat, he said.

—You alright?

—Tired.

—Come to bed.

He shrugged as best he could. Her shoulders slumped as she looked at him, dirty, on her couch. Maybe she was thinking of those nights he didn't come home, if he sat, filthy, on another woman's furniture. Maybe she remembered the way he smelled afterward, as though some of the mill had rubbed off on those foreign sheets, or those sheets onto him. He could wash and wash but there was always a residue Andie could detect and he'd see it in her eyes.

—I gotta work in a few hours anyway, he said.

—It's stupid. You working like this.

She picked her way to the kitchen. Her bathrobe caught a kernel of stray cat food and it rolled on the laminate, over and over, ticking like a moth. She brewed coffee – organic, shade-grown, fair-trade roast that cost him three dollars more per pound than it would've ten years earlier. You couldn't even get non-organic coffee anymore, unless you went instant, and Andie refused to drink instant. So Mitch forked out, to keep her happy, even though the guys at the mill gave him hell for it same as they had been for however many years. The world changed, Mitch figured, but people more or less stayed the same.

—There's oil on the gloves in the sink, he said.

—I'll wash them.

—You don't have to.

—I don't mind, Mitch.

He joined her in the kitchen and she brought him a ceramic coffee cup and the heat stung his fingers as he took it. The mug had a picture of an old friend, Will Crease, being punched in the gut by his dad. Its caption read: *You're not in Mayberry anymore!* Mitch had snapped the photo for that mug, at a family dinner after Will's dad came back from Kosovo. Those were better times, maybe. Andie folded into the chair nearest him and nudged her bathrobe closed around the lapel, but not before Mitch glimpsed skin.

—Luke's still not here, she said.

And that, his son, was just one more thing.

—When'd he leave?

Andie gave a half-hearted shrug.

—I guess I'll go look for him.

—It's almost morning. He'll be home or at work in a couple hours.

—You'd think he'd have the courtesy to call, Mitch said.

Andie dragged a hair behind her ear and he immediately regretted saying even that. She had her eyes fixed right on him, and after a second she reached across to touch his face – he'd bruised it slightly, caught a chunk of stray pine to his cheekbone. He knew what she must have been thinking: who was he to judge Luke for not coming home at night? Did *he* ever call? There was something so humiliating about being judged on par with a teenager, let alone your son.

—Want me to make breakfast? she said.

—I'll grab something from Tim's on the way.

She spun her mug between thumb and index. Mitch knew a joke about women who did that at a bar, but didn't mention it. She was never a touchy woman. He ran his finger along a gouge in the table and counted the knots in the grain. —If Luke comes home, he said, but couldn't bring himself to ask anything of her.

She glided to him and he felt her palm land on the back of his chair. Her nails *therrapp*ed the wood. Mitch curled his fingers around the mug and squeezed as hard as he could, until the heat needled his palm. Then Andie dragged her fingernails over his scalp and he closed his eyes and felt something like relaxation, if for just an instant.

—I'll let you know, she said, and kissed his forehead.

—I need to set things right.

She rubbed his cheek. Her smooth knuckles ground against his stubble and the warmth from that hand spilled into his cheek, the warmth from the mug into his palm.

AN HOUR LATER, Mitch's watch alarm woke him from a frail sleep. His head was in Andie's lap, her fingers dragging pleasant lines on his scalp. She told him he didn't have to go to work, that he had nothing to prove, and he hovered with his chin against his chest and his palms flat on the edge of the couch. He could get a lot done with even one day off work. But Mitch pulled his arms back and wiped a knuckle in his eye and cashed in on some last energy reserve. —That's not how it is, he told her.

Once beyond town limits he stopped at the Tim Hortons and got them to fill his thermos. The drive to the sawmill took him along a mountain ridge with Invermere and much of the valley beneath him in a well of darkness. The goats were out in force, more than he'd ever seen. They loitered at the roadside or straddled the yellow line, mouths grinding circles, and Mitch wove among them. Years back, in the days when Luke was still breastfeeding and they were so broke they sometimes ate dinner with his mom of necessity, he struck one of those goats with his Ranger. The creature barrel-rolled over his hood and landed on its knees in the box, all anger and not injured. After much baying and coaxing, Mitch phoned in sick because he couldn't chase the creature from his truck.

The road brought him through a hotel town called Radium, with major construction under way on a strip mall along its main drag. As he drove through, Mitch spotted his brother's truck, a forty-five-thousand-dollar enviro-friendly bio-dieseled no-footprint half-ton with *Cooper Contracting* decaled on the side. Nowadays Paul bid whole subdivisions, didn't work piecemeal jobs in satellite towns where his name wouldn't carry weight. And he no longer strapped on tools – just marched job sites with suits in tow, marked comments on blueprints, pupils like dollar signs.

Mitch pulled in next to the truck and scanned for Paul and spotted him in the doorway of the reno'd Liquor Depot, propping it open so two goons could haul drywall through. Mitch had a year and a half on Paul but his brother looked a decade younger, had good colour in his short hair. His features didn't sag and he kept a trimmed goatee that split his jaw in two. From profile, that scruff jutted from his chin like a hangnail. Paul wore the trademark coonskin hat tilted over his forehead – a relic from their boyhood years. Their dad donned that thing every time he trekked into the great outdoors, and, wearing it, Paul could have been Larry Cooper incarnate.

Paul saw him as he approached. The drywallers made a final pass and his brother stepped from the doorway.

They hugged like men.

—Been a while, man, Paul said.

—How's it going anyway.

—Comme ci, comme ça.

—Don't talk crazy to me, Mitch said, and Paul grinned.

In the background, saws whirred and men barked orders. The air smelled like tools.

—You look like you're about to die, Paul said.

—Worked a couple double shifts is all. On my way there for a triple.

—Time for a coffee?

Mitch pretended to look at his watch. He was rolling overtime, didn't need to show up if he wanted a day off, wouldn't be missed. —Yeah.

They rode Paul's half-ton a few blocks to a little shop

called the Daily Grind, off the main street among a row of old houses with great, sagging power cables. It was run by an old Ukrainian couple with wide smiles who lived above the shop. Mitch ordered a jelly donut and an empty mug and Paul asked for the usual and shoved Mitch out of the way to toss around his money.

They parked themselves in a far corner. The place was shelved full of fresh bread and black-and-white pictures of the old Ukrainian guy in different places around the world. Paul flipped open two different cellphones and shut them both off and rattled them on the table. He had a gigantic foamy coffee with whipped cream the guys at the mill would call a faggaccino.

—Awful job. I don't know why I took it in the first place, Paul said.

—Money.

—The owner, Norm, leaves a trail of slime when he walks, Mitch. How many hours you putting in, anyway?

—Did eighty-four last week.

—Why?

Mitch bit his donut and looked anywhere but at Paul. In grade school he once won a jelly donut for a math test and all the filling burst onto his shirt on the first bite.

—What else am I gonna do?

—Sleep, maybe.

—Can't. No, can't do that.

Paul pushed his fingertips to his temples. —You alright? Paul said, and Mitch felt him searching. —I thought she forgave you. Last time we talked.

—I've been thinking about Hunter lately, Mitch said.

—Mitch.

—Hunter was some dog. I remember when Luke was a year old and we went to Mom's for Christmas. He latched onto Hunter's coat and Hunter pulled him around the living room.

—How is Luke? Paul said.

—Seventeen. That's how he is.

Mitch sipped coffee straight from his thermos and Paul stabbed the foam atop his drink with a bamboo stir stick. When they were children, he and Paul swore oaths to each other never to drink coffee, or alcohol, or smoke cigarettes.

Then Mitch's cellphone rang and Andie's number came up on the call display. He flashed the screen to his brother and mouthed *ball and chain*.

—Luke's here, Andie said.

—How is he?

—The same.

—I'll come home.

—He won't stay, Andie said. —Hurry.

Mitch set his phone beside his brother's two and exhaled a long breath. Maybe he'd get a day off, after all. —I'm so tired nowadays, he said, staring at the table.

—He just needs some time. He's seventeen.

—I don't even see how it has anything to do with him.

—Dad hauled you from the cop shop when you were his age, Paul said with a wink. He sipped his fancy coffee and Mitch gulped the tar-like crap from his thermos.

—It's Andie too, he said. —We've talked and moved on but I see it in her eyes.

Paul tapped his temple, shrugged like a man who'd given things up. —Me and Vic. Well.

Mitch scratched his chin and then both he and Paul leaned back in their chairs, hands hooked behind their heads. Identical like brothers. Paul pocketed his two phones, one in each chest pouch like weird, square breasts. There weren't, Mitch realized, many people left who he could have a conversation with.

MITCH KNEW AS SOON AS he opened the door that Luke was gone. The house smelled like burning and he noticed the screen door open behind Andie, who sat at the kitchen table with her forehead against her wrist. Red, blobbed liquid seeped down the stove and pooled at its base. There was an upturned stainless steel pot on the floor and soup splatters on the cupboards and counters.

—I missed him, Mitch said.

—I spilled soup on the burner, Andie said, and cracked the knuckles in her fist. She stared at the kitchen table. Every sense in Mitch's body told him he was not welcome in that kitchen. —What took so long? she said.

—It's a bit of a drive.

—A bit of a drive.

Mitch eased a chair from under the table and its legs scraped the laminate floor. He abandoned that idea, put two hands on the back and stretched, as if aching.

—Andie? he said.

—I had time to make soup.

—That takes five minutes.

Dollops of soup had splashed onto the fridge and the microwave and if the situation were any different he'd have chuckled. Andie's eyes followed him around her kitchen. He snagged the paper towel roll from its holster under the cabinets and wiped the first gobs around the burner.

—Where were you? she said.

He tossed a sloppy wad in the garbage. —At the mill, he said, not understanding why he'd lie.

—Luke said –

—Couldn't you hear the saws?

—He quit his job.

Mitch shoved the garbage back under the sink and closed the door with his foot. It bounced back open and banged his shin. —Why'd he quit? Mitch said, and hunkered down on all fours to mop up the mess.

—I didn't ask. He wanted me to.

—Everything I do for him.

—He said he doesn't forgive you.

Mitch rocked onto his heels. He tossed another heap of soiled towels into the garbage. What the hell was he supposed to do about that? —For what? he said.

Andie had no response and wouldn't look at him when he tried to catch her eye.

—And why the *fuck* should that be any of his business?

Still, she would not look at him.

—He should get his own fucking life in line before he starts judging mine.

He heaved the garbage back under the sink and washed his hands.

—Andie, he said, looking out the window, and when she said nothing: —Andrea!

Her chair made a noise on the floor and he turned to find her staring at him. —I guess I'll go look for him, he managed. She nodded and he watched her, the way she ran her tongue along her teeth, the way she fiddled with her big toe when she was nervous. Of course he didn't deserve to be forgiven.

MITCH SEARCHED UNTIL he grew tired of the hopelessness. He'd been raised in Invermere and he thought he knew the hangouts: the barely upright fort down Caribou Road where kids got shitfaced; the gelati café off main street that was opened by a guy just out of highschool, who was now the mayor; the bakery, where he himself used to hang, where he once had a reputation as a good man. But Luke had his own haunts or he was hiding, or both. So Mitch went home and spent the remaining hours avoiding his wife and unsure why, until he registered the sound of her feet on the stairs, the tired creak of their boxspring that, at one point or another, she'd probably asked him to replace. Still, he waited on the couch, awake and dressed like a workman, knowing full well that he didn't have to, that she probably didn't even want him to.

When at last he joined her, he found Andie cocooned beneath their duvet. Mitch slid in next to her, fully clothed. Her hair spilled around the pillows and from the edge of the bed – where he slept now – he touched strands of it as though remembering. A breeze slipped through the open window and the temperature dropped, prickled his neck and the skin below his jaw. He felt his heat escaping, couldn't will himself to get up to close the window. Andie stirred, shifted toward him, and he slid his hand beneath her as she moved. She draped a wing of blanket over him. Her body was warm against his knuckles. She smelled like peach and orange, or something else fruity, a shampoo maybe. It smelled good.

The phone woke him. Andie rolled on top of him and blinked and for a moment there was space between those two rings, her palm flattened on his chest, him inhaling her breath, the way she prodded his feet with her toes. They were as close as they used to be, bodies curved, bodies enmeshed. Then a second ring shook through him and he fumbled over the night table. A pair of reading glasses hit the floor, some loose change rattled under his searching hand. His fingers found the receiver.

—Hello, he said.

—Mr. Cooper? a man said from the other end. The call display read BLOCKED ID.

—Yeah. Who's this?

—Constable Crease, Invermere RCMP. We've got your son in the drunk tank sobering up. He says you'll come get him.

The voice paused. Mitch listened to the silence. It'd been a long time since he talked to one of the Creases. Will, John, Ash – where did they even live? He'd gotten it backward, completely backward: the world *didn't* change, at least not much, at least not over one lifetime. But *people*? Christ, all he had to do was look at himself, there in the dark – both unforgiven and unwilling to *be* forgiven. Maybe some mistakes could never be set right.

—If not, the officer continued, —he can stay with us and you can get him in the morning.

Mitch glanced at the clock: two fifty-three a.m. —Hold on, he said.

He told Andie in four words that the cops had Luke. She leaned her head against the drywall. In the glow of the alarm clock, her hair draped around her shoulders.

—Leave him in the tank, she said.

Mitch watched her. His wife. —I'll come get him, he said into the phone.

Andie put her head back on the pillow and Mitch rubbed his eyes with the heel of his palm.

—It's cold, Andie said from the bed.

—I won't be long.

She poked her nose from beneath the covers. The skin on her arms glowed. There was nobody in the world more beautiful and he hated himself on such a fundamental level.

Mitch descended the stairs and threw on his jacket and his heavy boots and grabbed the remains of a six-pack from his fridge. Then he went out the door and climbed into his Ranger with its rusted door and missing tailpipe and tore a beer from its yoke. There were two ways to get to the detachment and he chose the longer one, past the school where a group of kids stood in a tight circle, a periodic flame bobbing between them. He finished his beer and tossed the empty out the window. He hit two of the two red lights in town and told God to fuck right off.

The detachment was a solid red brick building. His son and Constable Crease waited inside under a wall-mounted buffalo head. The officer had dark glasses, was shorter than him, seemed to tighten his jaw in that way a man does to shrug off bitter memories; they used to be best friends. Luke slouched in a chair.

—Hey Will, he said to the officer.

—Hey, Mitch, the officer said.

Luke didn't look half bad: red around the eyes, a little dirty. What Mitch expected from a kid out partying. —May as well get out of here, he said, and led the way to the truck, where he cranked the heat because it seemed so unnaturally cold for August. Luke hucked his pack in the box and hopped in the passenger side and stared out the window at nothing. After a bunch of random tuning Mitch got the classic rock station to play without static. They drove.

—You don't need to be embarrassed, Mitch said.

Luke shrugged.

—I don't care that you're a little drunk or stoned or whatever.

Luke placed his forehead on the window. His breath clouded the glass and he drew on the fog with his finger. —This isn't the way home, he said.

—That okay?

—I guess so.

—You know you can always call me. If you need a ride. Anytime. I don't mind.

—Okay.

They drove. Mitch fumbled with the radio when it went to shit and static blasted out the speakers. Luke didn't react to his fumbling or his discomfort and only shifted when a pothole bounced his head against the window. Mitch had to give up on the radio; he had to watch the road. Could nothing go right?

—I wish you'd have stuck around earlier. I just wanted to talk.

Luke half shook his head. —You're talking now.

—I guess I am.

They passed the school. The kids were gone. His beer can lolled in the wind at the edge of the road, near the ditch. He had two left. He could offer one to Luke.

—I don't know why you're mad at me.

—Yes you do.

—I just wish you didn't hate me.

—You don't get it, Luke said, his voice heavy with the drawl of marijuana. —I don't hate you. I'm disappointed in you.

His house appeared in the edges of his headlights. He'd built it himself, how many years ago, concrete through to shingles, and now it needed repair. Same as his family, maybe – something else he'd built that needed repair. Except Mitch knew he could fix the house, he loved fixing things, was good at fixing things, and he knew he could

never cause enough damage to bring it all down atop him.
—I'm disappointed in me too, he wanted to say.

The engine idled in the driveway and the headlights illuminated the flaking paint on the garage door. He needed to paint that, vaguely recalled Andie asking him to do it. Luke stepped out, swung his pack on his shoulder, and disappeared inside. Mitch killed the ignition and the headlights and pulled the e-brake, and then shifted the truck to first gear because the e-brake felt too loose to hold. He rested his hands on the steering wheel and stretched his fingers. The light in Luke's room flickered on and his son's head bobbed inside the window. One window over was the master bedroom, where Andie slept. In a few hours it'd be morning and Mitch would haul himself from bed, shove lumber until his muscles trembled and all that kept him from shutdown was some primal drive to work his way to redemption.

The Ranger's engine hissed in the August night. Mitch tweaked the key so the radio revived and he caught the tail of a nineties rock ballad. Luke's light went out and Mitch felt the evening air sweep through the rickety old truck, that relic of a truck. You go on and you go on – that's what Mitch knew. You go on and things work out or they don't but you keep trying, you keep on trying, because you have no other choice. He didn't leave the truck right away, just stayed in his seat and listened to rock songs from his youth and stared at those two dark windows.

ONCE YOU BREAK A KNUCKLE

The summer before Will finished university, he damn near broke a promise to his old man but came good on one to me – a childhood pledge to help build my first home. About the same time, a kid we knew from highschool forded the Sevenhead River and disappeared into the bush beyond, last seen wearing camouflage waders and gumboots and a Jack Daniel's trucker cap turned sideways. He was packing a 30-30 Winchester, pockets full of hollowpoints, and enough nautical rope to hogtie a grizzly. His motives were unknown. His potential to kill somebody was above average. Will's old man had been a cop longer than I'd been alive, and the Force assigned him to tracking the kid down. He asked me to help him, out in the bush, since I knew my way around the wilderness and since my own dad was once a bit legendary across the valley. Will's old man figured the two of us could shave days off a search, could *bag it and tag it* in no time at all, but all roads to Hell are paved with the best-laid plans, or so the saying goes.

When Will finally rolled through town – Inverhole, he called it – in early June, I was more than halfway done building my new house. I'd framed and sheeted the exterior walls, wedged up the load-bearers, and banged together some ladders between the floors. It only took me and Will a month to polish off the insides. I helped him plot circuits and measured sockets against my hammer, and he drilled holes through floor joists, in threes, for his electrical feeds. Will'd lost weight on the West Coast, but he was wiry as a devil. He only stood as high as my chest, but most people only stand as high as my chest. Growing up, what Will lacked in size he made up for with stubbornness. A few times he'd come home big-lipped, cheeks veining like a bloodshot eye. His old man used to think Will'd make a good boxer – he had the build to do well in lightweight, the build of a long-distance runner – but his knuckles were as brittle as onion skins. He broke three bones in his jab hand before his old man put the kibosh on the whole operation.

There were days when Will stomped around like a guy with something to win back. There were days I'd have fired him if he worked for me. He chipped four of my auger bits on nailheads. He sunk a hole straight through my styrofoam insulation and we had to patch it with blast-in fibreglass. Some days the temperature peaked over forty and we'd call a French advance and retreat to the basement where the heat couldn't kill us. This was 2009, with forest fires burning the Okanagan dry. The radio droned on and on about blazes skipping barricades and counter-fires gone rogue and a crew of bushworkers digging ditches to keep themselves alive. Nearly every half-hour, waterbombers filled their monsoon buckets in Lake Windermere, and in the evenings their distant engines made a sound like pissed-off wasps. It was an uncanny summer – the sky wouldn't darken or light up completely. Even in the dead of night it was all off-brown, like a puddle full of sawdust, the Purcells' upper ridge aglow. Flames bigger than cities nipped at the far side of those mountains, and you could never escape the feeling that warm air, as if from a car radiator, as if from a dog's breath, was blowing in your face.

WE FIRST HEARD ABOUT the missing kid midway through July. Will's old man showed up at the end of the afternoon in scuffed jeans and a T-shirt that said, *I Will Kick Your Ass and Get Away With It*. Me and Will were out on what would one day be my porch. We'd kicked up our feet on empty spools of fourteen-gauge wire. Piles of those things littered the place, like giant versions of the bobbins on my wife's sewing machine. That was Will's doing: he worked fast as the dickens but was piss-poor at guesstimating how much wire he'd need for any given room. Hence the empty spools. Smart and fast, but not second-nature – that's how Will Crease worked. He was studying to be a writer at the time, on the West Coast, but a few summers ago, in a rare moment of bared hearts, he told me he'd have turned cop if his old man didn't make him promise not to.

That day in July, Will's old man looked tired like only someone of his profession can. He wore dark sunglasses and a pair of Gore-Tex boots instead of steeltoes. A red-and-pink gash above his eyebrow drew my attention to his baldness. At a distance – or from most angles – John Crease looked like the kind of guy who'd either kill you in an alley or drag you from the pits of Hell. He was two-hundred-twenty pounds of old man strength. His cop's moustache was mostly grey, but immaculate. He called his fists "Six Months in the Hospital" and "Instant Death," and if you said something stupid he'd hoist them up and make you choose. Only when he took off his sunglasses did he show his age – or at least how bad his day had been. He did so that evening – took the sunglasses off – and hooked them in the collar of his shirt. Lines spread out from his eyes, down his chin. He seemed to be perpetually gritting his teeth.

He turned a wire spool on end and lowered himself to a sit. Then he waved toward the six-pack of Kokanee on the ground beside me. I flipped him one.

—You guys remember a kid named Duncan Jones? he said, and cracked the beer.

—Dragged me out of the Kicking Horse, Will said, referring to a whitewater-rafting trip with our grad class, eight years prior.

—Thought that was him, Will's old man said. He picked at the beer tab with a thumbnail. It *tink*ed, over and over, until he grimaced and twisted it straight off. —His family reported him missing today.

—He's our age, I said.

—I know that, Mitch.

—How long he been gone?

214

Will's old man shrugged, swung his gaze from me to Will, but Will just stared straight forward, hands behind his head, watching the sun sink below the Purcells. The sky had gone the colour of a rusty sawblade. Will probably liked the look of those mountains. We used to say they looked like breasts, even though that's stupid. As kids, me and him could pinpoint a cave on a rock face, noose-shaped and dark like a hole in the world. Maybe Will was thinking about how Invermere hadn't changed, since mountains don't change, not like the rest of the world. On the West Coast all he had was hippies and the ocean – and even the ocean is always moving around.

—Guys your age don't go missing, Will's old man said, eventually.

—Not by accident, Will said, and he slunk an eye sideways to look at his old man, whose tongue moved in a slow circle over his teeth, his face soured up like he had a point to make but didn't care to do so in public. The two of them weren't on speaking terms that summer, but hell if I was in the know.

—Girl trouble, I said. —That'll send you over the deep end.

Will's old man shot to his feet and booted an empty wire spool with a kick worthy of the CFL. Women: about the only thing those two talked about less than feelings. —Get so fucking tired of this job, Will's old man said. He stood there a minute, like he had something profound to add. Instead, he tapped my shoulder with his toe. —There any easy work to do, anything I can haul around?

215

—There's some ten-gauge upstairs, Will said.
—Need to move it down.

For a second his old man just loomed above us like a cop, like all the dirty secrets he knew about everyone – even me and Will. He pressed his fists to his lower back, where thirty years wearing an RCMP gunbelt had rubbed the muscles threadbare. Then he stomped off.

—He alright? I said, and Will, hands cupped behind his head, shrugged as best he could.

—We had an altercation, he said.

—What happened?

Will rocked forward, brushed his hands on his thighs in two brisk swipes. He could've been one of us right then, one of us small-towners, boys who hadn't and wouldn't move on from *the 'Mere*. He didn't have to be a university kid. —I'll tell you later, he said.

A floor above, Will's old man cursed and you could hear his boots clunk toward the stairwell. He probably had that massive roll of wire hugged to his chest like a body. Damned thing weighed near a hundred pounds, and that's why we'd left it upstairs for the night, since only a desperate idiot would steal it. Will cocked his head and smiled to himself – he and his dad were engaged in a lifelong game of one-upmanship, and who knows what kind of joke was whizzing through his head. Those days, me and Will might have been best friends, but he'd acquired his old man's knack for leaving things unsaid.

—Andie will have dinner ready, I told him. That's my wife, Andie.

Will dipped his head. —Ash gonna be there?

That's my sister. I said: —Fuck you, Will.

Beneath his ballcap Will grinned his mischief grin – the one he used to put on whenever he played horrible pranks on his dad, like when he taped plastic wrap over the old guy's bedroom doorway, like the time he weaseled himself into his dad's weight division at a judo tournament, just so the old guy could pin him to the mat.

—I drive a thousand kilometres for you and this is what I get, he said, sounding indignant, but it was all pretend. We'd outgrown the Code. Plus Will and Ash had been sleeping together for near eight years, and I'd already whaled on him for it, long ago – cracked him edgewise with a two-by-four so hard he couldn't lift his arm for a week.

—Remember when she dumped you, I said. —For that scrawny kid.

—I got her back.

—Will Crease: always gets 'em back.

He swiped at me but fanned it. Then he tugged his ballcap low over his eyes. In his Carhartts and steeltoes, reclined as he was, he could've been a spitting image of his old man, right down to the stubble tracing his jaw. Will'd done better than us all – got the best grades, got his university paid for, had some stories published someplace – but he was nowhere near to crawling from under the shadow of his dad. John Crease could cover a lot of distance just by walking a mile, or so the saying goes.

The house shuddered, as if releasing a sigh. From the

basement Will's old man hollered: —When are we gonna eat?

A FEW DAYS LATER Will came up with the idea for the pulley-swing. He wanted something to do after work, while we sat around drinking beer. The swing was simple: just a pulley and a swivel hinge that he fixed together and attached to a truss with a screw like you'd use to hang a punching bag. He looped an inch-thick rope over the wheel, measured it to centre. And just like that we had our own little carnival ride. We took turns seeing who could hold the other off the ground longer, our arms shaking like weightlifters'. One time Will hoisted me high enough to make me let go for fear of my fingers getting chewed in the wheel.

Ash came by to share beer and deliver news from Will's old man. She taught piano to elementary-school kids, but on the side she worked at the station, guarding weekend drunks. According to her, Will's old man had taken a police dog named Annabel, a great big German shepherd blind in one eye, and tracked Duncan Jones to a hill above the marsh, on floodplain from the Sevenhead River. There, he found leftover campfire and fistfuls of dried milkweed packed to a nest and what looked to be the antlers from a six-point whitetail – which was bad news, since it wasn't season. Duncan himself was missing in action, but Will's old man numbered the day a success. He loved dogs, though – all animals, really – so that's a given.

Ash brought a fold-out director's chair, a canvas thing, and she set it up while me and Will horsed around on the pulley. I could get Will spinning at a pretty good clip, since I outweighed him by thirty pounds. Ash wore dark cord pants and one of Will's few collared shirts that flopped sideways and showed some skin. She always donned the clothes Will hated just so they could argue about it. Her strawberry hair was tied in a braid and she tended to play with it while idle. There were three little scars on her cheek in a tight triangle like that one constellation, and a speck in her iris I don't know what to call except a speck. She pulled a page of the *Valley Echo* from her ass pocket and as she smoothed it flat I saw a grad photo of Duncan Jones, the headline: BROKEN HEART? Ash stared up at us past her eyebrows, her lips pulled to a pucker like a mom.

—Is this what you'd do if Andie left you? she said to me.

—Probably, I said.

—Will?

—As long as she didn't tell Mitch she was leaving me, I'd be okay.

—Fuck you, I said, and Will winked. Then he dropped the rope and crossed the room and sat down between Ash's feet. He put some weight on her knees. She nabbed his hat and flung it away like a Frisbee. On the West Coast Will played like the king of the wild frontier, swore to wear his ballcap even if he someday won a big award, if he ever got famous, but Ash had no time for it, the facade. She didn't like rednecks and idiots.

—I applied to the Force, Will said. He had his elbows on Ash's knees, and her thighs pressed his ribs. Her lips were pinched in a straight line, and looking at her, I had no idea what she thought or if they'd even talked. Will couldn't see her from his angle, but he relaxed with his weight on her legs. It was like he expected she'd take his side.

—Don't tell my dad, he added and gazed out over the unfinished balcony as he said so, out across Invermere. We were never the kids who ran the town – it never felt like ours, probably because none of us ever intended to stay. As it turned out, only Will escaped. The rest of us got claimed by the mill, or by our own dads' careers, or by girls. That's the small-town curse. It's not a bad life to have, don't get me wrong. But it's a life you should only choose after you've got the know-how to choose. My one regret, maybe. Right then, I had a flash of Will's old man when he found out Will was applying to be a cop – that special way he could pull his face to a scowl, that special way he could make you feel, right before he punched you.

—Your dad'll kill you, I said.

Ash said: —He'll choke you out, at least. And then he'll choke out Mitch for keeping it secret.

—Just don't tell him, Will said, looking from me to Ash and back again. —Don't *lie*. Just don't tell him the truth. *Omit* the truth.

—That's the same thing, Ash said.

—It's not.

—You want to ask your dad? I said.

Will smiled toward his hands, but it looked more like a grimace, like the face you make when somebody cracks a joke that reminds you of a dead person. —Dad and I aren't really talking, he said.

—I know.

—He wants me to keep at it, in Victoria. Do grad school. Be the first Crease to get a master's.

—What's so bad about that? Ash said.

Will shifted between her legs. He latched onto her knee and squeezed and she yelped, but before he could grin or enjoy it she twisted his ear, hard. They'd always been like that, so combative. And they argued about basically everything – but that's what Will liked about her, I'm sure of it. She could stand up to him, physically or otherwise. Once, on a roadtrip to the coast, they argued the whole way about churches and cults. Another time, Ash re-broke Will's collarbone when she knocked him down a set of icy stairs. They were just like Will and his old man, except for the obvious parts. I got the impression, watching them, that there was stuff Will wasn't telling me and stuff he never would.

—It's not *real*. What my dad does. That's real.

—I don't know about what you do, Will, I said. —Your dad thinks it's enough.

Will rubbed his jaw for a second, looked up at Ash as if to get support. She was playing with his hair, flat and egg-rimmed by the ballcap she'd whipped across the room. After a second of his gaze, she tweaked her eyebrows at him – *well?*

—You try having a cop for a dad, Will said, which pissed me right off every time he brought it up. It'd always been the opposite with my dad, rest his soul. He was a birdwatcher, a Parks naturalist, university educated, but he wanted us boys to land jobs you could have an arm-wrestle with. Not that it hasn't worked out for me and my brother, but sometimes you get envious.

—There's no rush, I said, but I'm not even sure what I meant.

—Everyone says that.

—Well maybe everyone's right.

Will's face twisted up, so disgusted – his unmatchable stubbornness heading its ugly rear. He gave me a limp wave, just the wrist moving, as if I wasn't smart enough to know how he felt, as if I were a dumb redneck and not his best friend since who knows how long. —You try having a cop for a dad, he said.

—I would, Will, except my dad's dead, I snapped.

—Guys, Ash said.

—Stop being a whiny bitch, I told Will.

He sunk against Ash, lolled his head over her knee. —You're right, he said toward the ceiling. Will could tell straightaway when he'd crossed a line, could defuse a situation like no one's business – something his dad taught him. The first weapon a cop employs is his mouth, Will's old man always said. The second weapon is an ass-kicking.

—I won't tell your dad – unless he flat-out asks.

Will flipped me a beer and cracked one for himself – a peace offer. —You're a good friend, Mitch. Possibly the best of friends.

—Fuck you too, Will, I said, and then we drank.

A couple days later, I took the day off working on the house so me and Will's old man could go do a search and scour for Duncan Jones. I left Will in charge, which under normal circumstances would be a mistake, but there you go. His old man had done the cop thing and found out Duncan Jones liked to camp at a place called Mount Tobias, in the Rockies. We headed off that way in his squad car, a Chevy Impala with the code name fifteen-Charlie-seven and a series of bullet-hole stickers on the driver door that he thought were cool. He'd brought the German shepherd, Annabel, and the beast panted away in the backseat. During the ride, Will's old man made the required joke about the criminal in the back who'd forgotten to shave, and then another about him getting dibs on the shotgun – the one stored in a rack right between the front seats – if it came to a firefight or a *tactical repositioning* from a grizzly. —I don't have to outrun the bear, he said to me, and winked, but I'd heard that one before.

We went as far as the road would take us. Will's old man let Annabel out, and the dog came and put some weight on my shins. I scratched her behind her ears. Then Will's old man removed the shotgun from its rack. —Because Duncan Jones was armed, he told me. I guess, as the saying goes, it's better to have what you need than need what you have.

Will's old man figured Duncan Jones wasn't a threat to anyone but himself, and maybe some of the poor animals who wandered between his irons. If a guy was going to go postal, he just went – that's what he told me. Guys like

Duncan, guys off the deep end, could be scooped back to shore with some gentle persuasion. When Will's old man said *gentle* he made quotes in the air with his one free hand. John Crease: the kind of guy everyone wants as a dad up until the point they do something stupid.

—You talked to Will at all? he said, holding a branch so it wouldn't whip me in the teeth.

—A bit, yeah, I said.

—He say anything?

—Anything about what?

—About *anything*, Mitch, Will's old man said, and let a little sigh follow the last word, and I felt pretty dumb right then, and then pretty terrified, because I might have to lie.

—He said you guys were fighting.

—We're not fighting, Will's old man said. He scowled at me, giving off all that menace as if he might just punch me right then and there. Not that he *would* punch me. Still, he looked like he might.

—Well, not talking, I said.

He scratched the nape of his neck. —He mention what his plans are?

—No.

—He doesn't want to do a master's degree, but the Force'll pay for it.

—Man, that's free money, I said, uneasily.

—He could stay in Victoria. The Force will *pay for it*, his old man said. —Maybe I could get transferred there.

We got going again. I was worried he'd know I'd omitted the truth.

224

In general, that summer, the forest wasn't in great shape. The place smelled like woodsmoke instead of pine needles and nectar and the air was dry enough for it to tickle your throat if you breathed too deep. I don't know a whole lot about ecology, but to my mind soil shouldn't be grey and it shouldn't powder your fingers like chalk. People said the hot spring and mild winter had caused more mountain meltwater than ever, but everything – the low, bent dogwoods, the knee-high bushes, even the falling pinecones that my head was like a magnet for – was parched, papery, brown.

Eventually Annabel perked up, and Will's old man tightened his grip on the shotgun. The dog veered off the path and bolted between the trees, not running, but fast enough that the two of us had to hustle. We must've been nearing the summit, where people camped all the time. As we bushed on through, I couldn't see ten feet forward, but Annabel's clumsy traipsing was enough to guide us. Will's old man held the shotgun in front of him, at an angle, and he used his elbows to ease branches and debris out of his way.

After another minute of fighting through the woods, the tree cover fell aside and the forest opened up into a glade with a great, wide panorama of the valley and the Purcells off on the horizon, white-capped like the teeth of the earth. The sky blazed like a chimney, but I don't know if that was from the fires or the afternoon sun gunning light through the haze. Six years earlier the same thing had happened, and most of the Interior got burned. A lot of people lost their homes. Invermere, and most of the Kootenays, had the Purcells as a shield, but if the fires wanted to scale the mountains, the fires would. It was pretty awe-inspiring, all that destruction, all that power.

Then Will's old man said my name in a slow, sober way that made me not want to turn around, not want to see whatever it was he'd discovered, because I'm not like Will's old man or even Will – I can't block things out like they can, I don't have the stomach for it. Most people don't, even though most people – at least most guys – like to say they do. But there's no way to test it. You just have to end up staring something awful in the face, and maybe not even something physically awful. Everyone regrets things, and to be a cop, I think, you need to be able to face that regret full on, or else it'll ruin you. Will's old man always said the job eats up your humanity. I still don't know what to tell him in response.

What he'd found was a decapitated stag's head, impaled on a tripod of sticks, its antlers sawed off and its open mouth stuffed to bulging with milkweed. It was a gruesome thing to look at, and then, looking at it, to smell – the eggy stink of gore and flies and that way animal guts stain your skin orange. The creature's eyes lolled into its head, probably where they went as it bled out. Its mouth had been forced open – I could tell by the rigid muscles in its cheek. It was like staring all dead things in the face.

Will's old man had taken off his sunglasses and hooked them in the collar of his shirt. The creases around his eyes bunched up, especially in the fatty bit above the cheek-bone. He loved animals so much. Annabel inched forward to sniff the stag's head, but even she seemed unnerved, or at least as unnerved as dogs get. Will's old man let the shotgun's muzzle touch the dry dirt, and with his free hand he pinched his temple, the bridge of his nose. —I'm sorry, Mitchell, he said.

—No.

He waved his hand at me – just the wrist, just like Will. —I'll call this in, he said, and pulled his shoulders back and straightened, cashing in on one last energy reserve.

And then a rifle blast cracked through the air.

It was close, so close, and as loud as a treefall or a light-ning strike or a backblasting car with no muffler. I felt the concussion of it, the *whoomp* of air, and then Will's old man clamped one massive hand on my shirt. He heaved me to the ground. I landed wrist-first, on my knees, felt the impact spike all the way to my shoulder. Will's old man yelled something, I don't remember what. The bushes were all shuffling, and the trees, and the dry grass shimmered in the air as if we were in some part of the Old West. Will's old man levelled the shotgun, pressed the stock to the meat of his shoulder. His whole upper body leaned forward, one foot braced, knees bent and calves quivering in anticipa-tion of the firearm's kick. His face was stone solid. His eyes squinched to bead points. He breathed slow, even, as if the adrenalin hadn't touched him. And he'd flattened me, effortlessly. People actually *fought* with that man.

A second shot barked from the forest, but there was no

flash, no sound of impact. It was a warning, a scare tactic; maybe no bullets were being fired *at* us. Will's old man hauled me to my feet and we bolted for the tree line, and then, without words, jogged down the path with Annabel taking point. Will's old man breathed in through his nose and out through his mouth in double-exhales, sweat pearling at his temples and on the ridges above his eyes. He looked like he was clenching his teeth. Somewhere during the run his sunglasses had shaken loose from the collar of his shirt.

—Fuck sakes, he said when we reached the car. Sweat had turned the neck of his shirt grey, and his cheeks were flushed red, burning. He pressed both of his fists to his lumbar, knuckles first, and he sucked a steadying breath, as if to ignore a great discomfort. Then he opened the rear door and leaned on it while Annabel clambered inside.

—You can't even help anyone anymore, he said.

He'd misjudged the situation and was probably hating himself for it, would be slow in forgiving himself. That's how things went, how they always had: he held grudges for a long, long time, and he could just as easily hold one against himself. He eased the door shut, making sure Annabel's tail was clear of the latch, and then he put his hands on the top of the squad car, spoke right at me: —It's like nothing you can do will change a thing.

He *therrap*ed his fingers on the roof. After a moment of that, of me looking anywhere but at him while his fingers thrummed, he pushed away from the car and lowered himself in. Annabel loosed a low, throttling whine from

228

her throat. I'm not sure if Will's old man wanted me to say anything, or what I could possibly have told him to make things okay, but not a day passes when I don't wish I had gathered the nerve to try.

IT ISN'T EASY TO sleep after getting shot at. Take that from someone who knows.

Will's old man stopped at the foot of my driveway and the two of us sat in the idling car and stared at the lights and the windows of my house, listening to the radio play who cares what. He stuck his fingers through the ringwire grate that separated us from Annabel, and the beast set about licking them. We hadn't said a whole bunch on the way home. Will's old man had reports to file, questions to answer – the Force might be in touch, he'd told me. It was the time of night when everything turns the same shade of grey. The dying hour, I'd heard it called.

—If you see Will, don't tell him what went on, he said.

—You got it, Mr. Crease, I said, and climbed out of the squad car. He waited for me to get inside before driving off – thirty-eight percent of all assaults happen while people fumble for their keys. I had a missed call from Ash and another from Will, but neither left any messages. I didn't call them back because the last thing I needed to hear was that Will had drilled through another plumbing line or blown up the breaker panel or cut off his own hand with a tigersaw.

Andie had ordered pizza and left them on the coffee table and hit the rack early, so I ate straight from the box, turned on the TV and listened to a repeat of some Liberal politician touting the slogan *It Can't Hurt to Try*. I didn't exactly care to hear about the war or the economy. All I could think about was the gunshot and Will's old man pushing me to the ground. It was like I could taste the sulphur, somehow, or the smell of cordite, but of course I'm imagining that. Still, it got my heart racing. I don't know how anyone faced those kinds of situations days out and days out. That doesn't make me a coward. That makes me normal. The line between being brave and being stupid is thinnest at both ends, or so the saying goes.

I checked in on my wife. She had our hot water bottle hugged to her chest and some of the liquid had spilled across her and probably made the evening heat bearable. Then I grabbed a yoke of three Kokanees from the fridge and headed for the beach. About everybody I know likes the beach at night, and even though the sign says it closes at ten, the cops won't kick you off if you don't cause a ruckus. One time, when me and Andie were first dating, I brought her there and spelled out her name with tea lights in the sand. It seemed like a good idea until a motorboat made a wave that put them out all at once, but maybe that was pretty cool itself. Later, a cop named Berninger found us and gave a sharp *tsk*, but we weren't causing a ruckus.

I cut along a dirt path that brought me around the rim of the gully, not because it'd get me to the lake any quicker but because I'd pass by my new house, still in its skin-and-bone state. I'd be a liar if I said it didn't make me proud, that house. Just seeing it gave me a tingle in my chest, in that spot right above the gut. Three thousand square feet, a good size for a family. My dad helped pay for it – said he owed me, from when I helped him build his own home, putting in sixteen-hour days for two bucks an hour, way back when I was thirteen. He slapped a sweaty cheque in my palm, for a wedding present. Twenty-five thousand dollars.

I thought I'd drink one of the beers on the porch, since that way I could stuff the other two in my pockets and be less conspicuous if I bumped into a cop. Not that they'd take them away. But when my house came into view I saw flashlights on the upper floor, zipping around as if searching the nooks and crannies. Fucking thieves. Probably the hicks – the same rednecks I'd been fighting since grade seven.

If I went in solo I wouldn't stand a chance. Usually I'd go get Will and we'd take a beating and hopefully dish one out, but I had no idea where he was, even if I figured it'd be with Ash, and she lived across town anyway. I couldn't even call the cops, hadn't brought my cellphone. Right then, I felt like an idiot kid again, like when I was thirteen years old without a place to go in the world. That time, I'd ended up going to Will's old man, which, as I watched those lights in my house, in the house I'd built and paid for from scratch, was the only place I could think to go.

He lived a couple streets down. It was twelve fifty-two when I reached his yard, and I knew he drifted asleep way earlier than that, on the couch, watching whatever movie happened to be playing on satellite. I knocked once and heard rustling, the unmistakable *thump* of their tomcat hitting the carpet, and then Will's old man peered through the slatted living room blinds, scowled like only he can, and came to the door.

—What is it, Mitch? he said. He wore grey Nike sweatpants and a T-shirt with a picture of two bears in bandanas eating human bones. The caption read: *Don't Write Cheques Your Body Can't Cash*.

—Sorry, Mr. Crease, sorry to wake you.

—Couldn't sleep anyway.

—I saw lights at my house.

—Lights? he said, and when he did it sounded so stupid, even to me.

—Like, flashlights, I said.

—You think there's someone up there?

—I got my tools in the basement.

—What're they worth?

—I don't know.

He scratched the nape of his neck, his whole arm moving in a circle above his head, looking old in a way I couldn't pin down. Maybe that ratty T-shirt made him seem frail, who knows. He blew a long, tired sigh out his nose and opened the door enough for me to step through. —Let me get some pants, he said, and waved me in. As he walked away I saw one arm bent at his hip, fist pressed to lumbar, and he shuffled his feet as he climbed the stairs to his bedroom. Operational police work is a young man's job – that's what he always told Will. It's a career with an expiry date.

He came downstairs in jeans and socks and sandals,

with his handcuff key chain in one palm, and he flipped the keys in the air and caught them without looking – a trick him and Will perfected years ago when they did judo together. He jerked his chin at the door. To the west, you could trace the outline of the Purcells – silhouettes against the dark tungsten sky. Will's old man tugged the door shut, and then he turned and faced those mountains, his chin raised and his eyes squinted, as if staring something down.

—We're going on evac warning, he said, but not in a way that invited me to comment. He did his cop's shrug. Then he stretched, probably to ease a knot in his lumbar, and I imagined those muscles of his untangling like galley ropes. I stood a full head taller than him but it felt like looking up.

The street lamps are far and few between in Invermere. We walked in darkness. Only the spill from living rooms and porch lights lit our way. Will and me used to hike around Invermere's dead streets at night, when the air smelled like paving salt and pine needles and lake. Since Will left I didn't have so much time to just walk around doing nothing, and even less since I got married. I suppose that's the way things go. Part of me wondered if Will's old man might not mind walking in the dark.

My house wasn't far off – in the daylight by now it'd have been in sight, or at least the roof would've.

—Is Will going to marry your sister? Will's old man said.

—*He is?* I said, coming to a stop.

—No, I'm wondering.

—What'd he say?

—He never said.

—Well, they've been sleeping together for like ten years.

—Jesus, Mitch, Will's old man said, this look on his face as if to say *what the hell*, as if he might headbutt me. Then a beam of light flashed around my house's second floor and Will's old man snapped his eyes away to look at it. He ran his tongue along his teeth. —Don't you keep your tools locked up in the basement?

—Yeah.

—Wonder what we're gonna find, he said with a little grin.

We kept on. Part of me hoped to find rednecks there so me and Will's old man could beat them pulpy, maybe smack them with his elbows – the hardest impact point on the lower arm. I have a history with the rednecks. Will's old man used to bitch about the justice system, until he got worried me and Will would turn into vigilantes. He might not have been unjustified in that fear – the two of us got in our fair share of scraps, and our dads had to spring us out. Will never got special treatment for being a cop's son.

—The kid, Duncan, Will's old man said all of a sudden. —He tried to kill himself, this evening.

—Why?

Will's old man stopped again, at the foot of the driveway. —That's what I like about you, Mitch. Everybody else asks *how*.

—Thanks, I said, but I'm not really sure what he was getting at.

—Know a girl named Vic Crane?

—Her dad's an electrician.

He rubbed the back of his neck. —Well, she saved his life, he said, and did his cop's shrug, and that was that. Then he put his hand on my shoulder and I looked right at it. Those hands of his – I've never seen any part of anybody that took such a beating. Once you break a knuckle, he always said, you will break it again.

—Don't let Will throw his life away.

—Okay, I said.

—You're a good friend, Mitch.

My house had no doors installed yet. Will's old man used his cellphone to light our way over the empty wire spools and other stuff that could make a racket. For an old guy, he glided around.

When we reached the stairwell he raised a finger to his lips and we listened in the darkness. I heard a squeaking sound, like a rusty teeter-totter. Will's old man cocked his head, bent his arms to half-guards – ready, I guess, in case one of us got jumped. All me and Will kept on the second floor was drywall and bags of fibreglass insulation – pink plastic packages big as couch cushions. I used to know a guy who stuffed his boots with that insulation.

Then a great Jesus *ka-thoomp* shook the house from upstairs, in the master bedroom. Will's old man gave a nod, like in cop films before guys storm a room. We went up. And there was Will and my sister, in the master bedroom, playing with the pulley-swing. Not fucking, thank the Lord – I'd rather get shot than see that. Will had his end of the rope coiled and he twirled it round and round so Ash whipped about the pivot at forty-five degrees. Her red hair was flung loose near her shoulders.

Will saw us standing there, let my sister slow down and drop with a *thump* to the plywood. She put a hand on his shoulder, probably not for balance. Will had this smug little smile on his face – almost a frown, actually, as if only half his face dared grin. His old man leaned on a stud and it creaked so he scowled at it.

Everyone stared at each other as if we were in a Western movie. Then Will's old man snorted. —Mitch thought he was being robbed, he said, and I damn well expected him to smack me. —I thought we'd find you guys sleeping together.

—In my brother's bedroom? Ash said.

Will's old man yawned, his big mouth opening wide. He sat down on a wire spool and brushed his hands over his thighs in a pair of slow, methodical swipes, his whole body – arms, shoulders, even his back – stretching with the action.

—I've got beer, Will said, nodding to a flat of Kokanees near the exit to the unfinished balcony. He flipped on a pair of halogen work lamps that lit the room amber, like a great big candle. —Was going to try and seduce Ash with them.

She belted him, and good on her.

I leaned on a sawhorse and Will tossed me a drink and I fumbled it and left it to sit so it wouldn't foam up. He and Ash had that look about them – not exactly sweaty but almost there, not red-cheeked but somehow blushing.

They sat shoulder to shoulder. If it were anyone but Will and my sister, I'd have left them be.

—We got shot at today, Will's old man said, his eyes on the plywood.

—Where? Will said.

—Up Mount Tobias. Was probably Duncan.

—Jesus.

—That's all I need, another hole in my chest, Will's old man said. He meant it as a joke but nobody even giggled. Will slurped beer suds and watched his old man, who didn't stop staring at the floor. They barely ever looked at each other at the same time, that summer. A confrontation was brewing, anyone could see it. It'd been brewing for a while.

—I want to join the Force, Will said.

—You think I don't know that?

—Crossed my mind.

—*Why?* Will's old man said, but there'd be no answer to that. He'd played all his cards, spent so long and done so much to get Will *out*, to get Will *happy*, and he knew – Christ, he knew – that Will's happiness would fly right out the window when he strapped on his first gunbelt. Ash rubbed her hand up and down Will's spine, the only support she'd shown. Will and his old man each chewed their lips, and at two different moments their eyes flickered to me, and I had this horrible feeling that they wanted me to take a side. Which they did, of course – I was the closest thing to a brother or a second son they had. Mitch Crease, they'd both called me, on separate occasions, growing up.

Then Will's old man noticed the pulley-swing. He waved his arm at it. —So what's this thing?

—A pulley, Will said.

—For what?

—Tug-of-war.

Will's old man laced his hands behind his head. —That so?

—Yeah, Will said, crossing his arms and getting into it. —That's so.

Even as he finished, his old man rose to his feet, wandered to the pulley, and took hold of one end of the rope. He gave a slight jerk, as if to appraise its worth. —You got what it takes, boy? he said, a devious twinkle in his eye.

Will stepped up. His old man rolled his neck around his shoulders and if it were an action movie you'd have heard the vertebrae crack. He adjusted his grip on the rope and Will did the same, and their hands and arms tightened until that thing went taut. Will's old man had the weight advantage by damned near seventy pounds, but Will had his unmatchable stubbornness.

—This is out of our league, Ash said to me, and gripped my arm as if to pull me away. She was dead right. The pressure in the air was tectonic. We sat down on the porch – not even in the same room – shoulder to shoulder, and I felt the evening wind rush past us and wondered what exactly was at stake.

I shouted the go-ahead, and in unison Will and his old man dropped a few inches, knees bent and their whole bodies straining. Their arms barely moved: father-son, sweating pearls and wearing beer-grins. Happy as ever, it looked like. You could see their determination. Will's old man had been shot, bludgeoned, once had both his shoulders popped from their sockets when he held three grown men on a rope ladder. But the way his teeth grit and his lips peeled over his gums – it was as if this stupid test was *the* standard to measure a guy's worth. Will looked the same. His arms were tenser than the rope. His face squeezed together around his nose, and his cheeks reddened even in the amber working light.

I could have watched that tug-of-war forever. It seemed like nothing would happen. They were so even, the two of them. Then Will's old man yelled out – a guttural, barbaric sound, a sound like you'd make to benchpress a car – and he heaved like I never knew a man could heave. Will flew straight into the air. He really flew. It was like something out of a Shakespeare play. His arms snapped above his head and his body just glided on up. And his old man kept the heave on. Yell, heave, flight – the whole thing lasted maybe a second, but I remember it in detail: Will's old man with his whole face bending inward and this wild amusement in his eyes; Will not even registering the fact of his ascent; the *ca-REAK* of the ceiling truss as it fulcrumed the weight of Will's whole body. I remember it in slow motion. And then *like that* Will was lodged two knuckles deep in the pulley-swing.

He flailed mid-air and yalped and swore and it took a moment for his old man to compute the mechanics of the situation. When he did, he dropped the rope, straight up fumbled it, and Will fell like deadweight. He spewed curses I had never heard. Ash bolted to him. He clutched his maimed fist and his old man kept distant, gazing at his own hands and his arms and the pulley – as if he'd come out of a trance, as if these things he trusted so much had at long last failed him.

—Will? his old man croaked, and stepped forward. I did too, came up behind Ash. The first two fingers of Will's left hand – his jab hand – bent sideways, toward the palm, and the knuckles rose above their sockets, black and blue and flattened in places they ought not be flattened. When he saw that hand, Will's old man went blood-white. He stood there above his son as awkward as a boy. He picked at the hem of his shirt, tugged it down, over his gut and belt. Will squinched his eyes to slits. I can't imagine how much that must've stung, and I've had my share of stuff like that.

And then in the next moment Will's grimace bent to a grin – his fucking mischief grin – and his eyes opened and he laughed. That's right – he laughed. He laughed like a guy does when he's suffered a wound that won't kill him. And that quick his old man went from sombre-face to shit-eating and, hell, so did I. Smiling like idiots, all of us. Well, except Ash, but behind every injured man is an unimpressed woman, or so the saying should go.

We all looked at it again: swelled up now, like a baby's hand. —I guess you win this round, Will grunted to his old man, who knelt in front of him and rolled up the sleeve so he could inspect it and, about as tenderly as I'd ever seen, cupped that mangled hand in one big, creased palm.

ME AND ASH WENT to get my truck, and some ice packs, and to let Will and his old man go at it, since enough had happened for the two of them to have an actual conversation. Not that I thought they'd work anything out – they were each too stubborn to yield, too much alike.

—You gonna marry Will? I said to Ash as we walked along the same dirt path I'd taken earlier. She was drunker than I expected, her footing erratic but not unsure, even though the path pitched and dipped at random.

—I don't know, she said.

—Ash, I said, and touched her arm. Below us, the gully spread out to the edges of vision, into the darkness beyond the spill of house lights.

—We talked about it.

Ash Crease, I thought, had a weird ring to it. And I couldn't get my head around the concept of having Will as a brother-in-law. When we reached my place I gave Ash the keys to my truck so she could get it started, and then I snuck inside to grab some ice packs from the freezer. I didn't want to wake Andie, because there'd be too much explaining to do and because we needed to get Will to a hospital one way or another. I heard my truck start with a cough – Ash not giving the glowplugs enough time to heat.

I took two ice packs and went to the truck. Ash had rolled it onto the road in neutral and swapped to passenger, lowered her window down and almost finished a smoke. Under the amber light of a street lamp, she looked way older than me – but that's the kind of effect amber light has, don't get me wrong.

—So big brother doesn't think I should marry Will, she said. She flicked the cigarette out the window, and I realized I had some kind of chance, right then, to change things, to not let Will throw his life away. And I knew, I knew, exactly what that chance would cost me.

—Is it a good idea? I said.

She gave me a devilish look, with just one eye and with half her mouth tilting to a smile. —Marrying Will, or your idea that I shouldn't?

—Both.

—What do you want me to say? Will's still a boy.

I chewed on that one for a second. —His old man thinks you're going to get married.

—I'm not sure Will's dad is an authority in this matter, she said.

We got quiet. My tires kicked up pieces of the asphalt because the roads were in disrepair. You could hear bits clanging around the wheel wells. The sky was brown and the rim of the moon looked like the edges of old paper. The air smelled of soot, and so did my truck.

—Will'd kill you, Ash said after a while. —If he found out what you're trying to do.

—I'm bigger than him.

—Mitch, she said, not in the mood to joke.

—He'd never talk to me again.

—But you're willing to risk that?

I thought about the two of them. Will was smart enough to get promoted through the RCMP ranks, and pretty quick. They'd make a down payment on a house big enough to raise a family, or Will would hand me the blueprints to a home he'd designed himself, and he and I would go at it – our childhood pledge. His old man would retire to grand honours, with a long-service award and so many people lining up to clap him on the shoulder – Corporal John Crease, more a legend than even my own dad, rest his soul. Will's old man would sell his home and he and Will would add a grandpa suite, and there he'd settle, while his son levelled drunks with his maimed jab hand, scoured forests for missing kids, and himself got shot at, himself felt that pulse of fear and dread that his old man must have felt so goddamned often.

—Why does it seem like I have to take a side? I said.

—I don't know. Why does it?

—I just want everyone to be happy.

She nodded like she understood. She nodded like I'd made a point. We rounded the corner to the road where my house was, and Ash reached out and patted me on the leg. —You're a good friend, Mitch.

—Everyone says that, I said, feeling sour.

I CAME UP THE stairs to my master bedroom with the ice packs in hand. The truck idled in the driveway, and I could all but picture Ash smirking as I tiptoed away. Will and his old man hadn't seen me yet, and I got a rare look at them as they are when no one else is around. They sat side by each on wire spools, shoulders slumped and wrists on their thighs, elbows flung wide and knees damned near knocking. They were grinning like guys with no reason not to. Man, Will would've ditched everything for Ash, banged together a life in good old Invermere, in the shadow of the Rockies and in the shadow of his dad. Things I kept him from: marriage, two boys who'd grow up to call me uncle, a gunbelt to rub his muscles threadbare, our friendship lasting to the end of days, to the moment of some head-on collision in a mountain pass – all the stuff his old man didn't want for him.

Will and his old man could have been the same guy from two different moments in time. Their talk was all murmurs and sudden bursts that made them go red-faced with guffaws. I missed my own dad right then, and I missed days like these with Will and his dad, looking forward in time or something, just the bullshit of it. You don't need to be a wise man to predict matters of the heart, or so I say. Behind them, the sky had turned the colour of plywood, and I realized Will and his dad looked about as happy as ever and that I hoped that would never change.

ACKNOWLEDGMENTS

I owe a debt of thanks to a great many people who invested a great many hours in the shaping of these stories – first among them Jessica Lamothe, who suffered the rough drafts of all but two (and damned near sixty others), and Anna Smith, who raised her fists in my defence over four years of undergraduate creative writing workshop.

Andrew Cowan lent (lends?) me his expert editorial eye, his scathing wit, and his non-stop constructive abuse. Thanks, too, to my classmates at the University of East Anglia for their thorough and thoughtful feedback, especially Joshua Piercey, Armando Celayo, Ellie Wasserberg, and Ben Lyle – their books are a-coming, take note.

The Gentlemen's Fiction Club fills a certain gap of literariness and expat camaraderie in what is otherwise a cold, grey city. Shout-outs to Hal Walling, Trevor "Chest" Wales, Rosie Westwood (honorary gentleman), and Annabel Howard (honorary expat).

My agent, the effervescent Karolina Sutton, deserves special mention for tolerating my hijinks and for somehow getting me published. On that note, I'm grateful to Nick Garrison and Helen Garnons-Williams, my editors, for their tireless enthusiasm. I'd also like to thank the people at Booktrust and the BBC National Short Story Award for becoming my unofficial champions here in the Old Kingdom and beyond – it means a lot.

Versions of some of these stories have appeared in *Grain, PRISM, Prairie Fire, Southword, The Malahat Review* and the BBC National Short Story Award 2011 anthology. In particular, thanks to John Barton and Rhonda Batchelor of *The Malahat* for publishing my first story and for subsequently inviting me to the fiction board. They're career-launchers, those folk.

The legendary – if not mythological – Bill Gaston bestows me with his blessings, editorial and otherwise, upon request, and the sheer calibre of these blessings is rivalled only by the calibre of his beer guzzling.

Lastly, and most obviously: my heartfelt appreciation to Lorna Jackson, who saw in me some spark of potential and set about nurturing it for four full years. She's a mentor, an inspiration, a friend.